I0567036

Tillamook

Burn

by

Albert Drake

Flat Out Press

ACKNOWLEDGMENTS: Some of the writings in this collection have previously appeared in the following publications:

"The Chicken Which Became a Rat". *Northwest Review*, and reprinted in *Best American Short Stories 1971*.

"Ambush". *Windsor Review*, and reprinted in *Michigan Signatures*.

"Conversation with my Father" and "Memory: Returning to an Empty Intersection," *Trace*.

Collage & Photos supplied by Albert Drake

"The 'Thirties as Allegory," *Sumac*.

"Tillamook Burn," *3 Northwest Poets* and *Rouge River Gorge*.

"The Summer of the Sad Cars," *Cutbank* #2

"Beyond the Pavement," *The Fault* #11

"Listening to Marty Robbins Sing White Sport Coat 20 Years Later," *Pebble*.

Library of Congress CIP Data: PS3554.R19T5 813'.5'4 77-14012

ISBN: 0-936892-26-9

Originally published by Fault Publications
Second Edition by:
Flat Out Press
PO Box 66874
Portland, OR 97290-6874

www.flatoutpress.com

Contents

Listening To Marty Robbins Sing White Sport Coat 20 Years Later 4

Beyond the Pavement 2

Memory: Returning To An Empty Intersection 19

Lents: Early Sunday Morning 22

Sunday Night 24

The 'Thirties as Allegory 25

The Chicken Which Became a Rat 26

Conversation with My Father 51

Tillamook Burn 53

Ambush 55

The Summer of Sad Cars 58

At Mt. Hood. Ledge. (July '38)

Listening To Marty Robbins Sing White Sport Coat 20 Years Later

For My Children

In your sleep the room is breathing,
ragged but untroubled, and I watch your cameo
faces white with winter against pillows
wondering: what are your dreams

As I wonder at those blurry snapshots
of my father, dead at thirty-nine,
an old man I thought, not interested
in a hell of a lot: what did he want

I still wonder, knowing years from now
you will look at photos, see me frozen
against some dim background, a fixed smile,
eyes reflecting the camera,
and wonder the same question.

Music evokes associations; photos fix time.
If poetry has a purpose it is as souvenir,
offering, journal, and tonight I offer
this poem against the future, to tell you

I never had a white sport coat, pink carnation –
what I had when I first heard that song
was eighteen years and a terrific fear
that someday I would be twice that.
I'm puzzled how it happened: simply
by breathing, in and out. It happened.

Beyond the Pavement

When they pulled into Swede's, the sun reflected with midday heat from every broken windshield and smashed fender. They had been to AAA Auto Parts, Johnson's, Sonny's Wreckers and two backyard junkers whose places had no name, and now the repetitious process of the search had become boring for Chris.

He had left the house hours before with a sense of excitement, the taste of toast and milk-coffee imprinted on his tongue and as the cycle had roared away from home he had felt the mounting sense of anticipation: his face reflected in the chrome gas cap, his father's body pressing against him, the sun glancing off traffic, people heading on this Saturday morning for Copeland lumber yard, Lents Hardware, Fred Meyers to do things. He loved the odor of gas, of oil boiling off the hot engine; he loved to go with his father on Saturday mornings to the junk yard, to play among the shattered wrecks. But now, as they pulled into Swede's A-l Parts, he was hot and tired and hungry.

His father gunned the engine and turned off the key as Chris jumped to the ground, avoiding the finned barrels and the exhaust pipes which cast shimmering heat waves. His bare feet hit the hard dirt and he walked carefully among broken glass, rusty metal, black mounds of parts. He had meant to put on his shoes before leaving home but his father had said, "That's ok, we'll be right back!"

They walked past the high board fence into the yard; in the center was an ancient house, sections of weather-beaten paint exposed between rows of hubcaps, license plates, radiator plaques, and all around were wrecked autos, settling hip high into the grass. On the oil-stained trail they met a man wearing a black skull-cap who carried a piece of metal on a wire, like a fish.

"Hiya, Mel," his father said.

"Hiya, Howard," the man said, smiling to show he had no teeth. "Hiya doing?"

"Can't complain."

They entered the dark building where heaters and headlights and radios, rows of metal bins, stacks of boxes of gears, door handles, switches, pistons spread in a confusion that spilled past doorways and blacked windows.

Behind a wooden counter saturated with the oil of years Swede rubbed a bearing with a cloth; he wore a leather apron, and his blonde hair was shaved from the tops of his ears down so that the shock of his head stuck up like some wild, profuse plant. "Hiya, Howard."

"Hiya, Swede. How's business?" His father leaned against the counter, pushed his white carpenter's cap back, and the hand strayed to his shirt pocket; he shook Bull Durham into wheat straw paper, licked and folded it with smooth motions. The match flared blue against the darkness, and then Chris saw the old man in the corner on a front seat which was now a sofa.

"Not bad. Price of scrap's going up; on the other hand a lot of people want to buy new cars figuring on a war. So it's about even-steven." He laid the bearing beside three others, wrapped them in a rag, and put them on the shelf. "Gotcher helper today."

"Yar, the squirt's ok," his father said, reaching to scuff Chris' hair. "We'll make a mechanic of him."

"Anything I can do you out of today?" Swede asked, wiping his hands.

"Yar, I need a U-joint for a '30 Hudson 8," his father said, his voice becoming serious, the cigarette bobbing on his lower lip as he watched Swede's face.

Swede rubbed his hands with the rag, impassively studying the bench top while in his mind he reviewed the cars, the boxes and bins and piles of parts assigned no categories for long ago he had realized that there was no way to organize the random parts; a man would go crazy trying to keep things straight. "A thirty," he said, spitting, "Yar, got one back here I think." He disappeared behind a curtain of tailpipes and Chris could hear him moving around and then he appeared with an orange box which he polished on his shirt front.

His father turned the box over in his hand, as if weighing it. "I got a job starts Monday morning. Up on the Columbia where they're building the dam, if I can get the ole Hudson to get me there."

"Would that be CCC or WPA?" Swede asked.

"Hell no, that's Corps of Army Engineers, that's a big project," his father said, taking a last puff on the cigarette and dropping the wet misshapen butt to the floor where he squashed it under his boot. "I get on there I'll be on easy street. No more bread and gravy." Nevertheless, he slid the orange box across the counter. "Got a used one of these?"

Chris looked up in dismay; this is what they had spent the entire morning searching for and now his father rejected it. He looked away, saw the old man on the car seat in the corner wrap one hand around the other and then shift them, like a flower in continual stages of unfolding. "Too many," he kept saying, "too many all the time."

"Be better by a mile to put in a new one," Swede said. "Those needles just don't last when they're wore. Not worth your time otherwise."

"You're telling me," his father said, smiling, pulling his cap bill to eye level, tucking in his shirt. "But I got more time than money. Anyway, I'll probably get rid of it soon, get me something newer. I'll keep that part in mind though." He took Chris's hand within the horny shell of his own. "C'mon, kiddee."

They walked the maze of bent and mangled autos and climbed on the Harley. It fired first kick and before Chris could ask why he had not bought the U-joint they were in the flow of Saturday noon traffic, both lanes of 82nd filled with cars. The next wrecking yard was Honest Abe's Auto Rebuild and when Chris's foot touched down it was on hot asphalt. Honest Abe's yard was the exact opposite of Swede's: the parking area was paved, the board fence was painted white and straight as a ruler; on the roof was a Bantam coupe, an advertisement, with Honest Abe SU 6779 on the door. They entered a lobby and Chris felt the cool tiles beneath his feet. Here everything was neatly racked and much of it was new: radios, fender skirts, fog lights, lap robes, and accessories.

"Yes, sir, may I help you?" The man wore a shirt and tie beneath his gray shop coat.

"Yar, I need a U-joint for a '30 Hudson 8". The man moved to the catalogue, wet his thumb, and began to look it up. His father said, "That'd be a used joint."

When the man closed the catalogue and shook his head, Chris's father said: "I thought I seen a '30 Hudson in the yard– ok if we take a look?"

"Sorry, sir," the man said, leaning against the counter on folded arms. "We can't allow anyone in the yard except employees."

"Nerts." His father pulled the cap brim down and Chris had to run to keep up with him. "Damn hebe," he said, kicking the cycle to life; Chris climbed onto the hot cycle tank, feeling annoyed and bored, thinking of all the things he could be doing at home, but he felt a little better when his father said: "Whatdya say we get a cup of joe?" .

They cruised down 82nd to Foster and turned right, just past the new Fred Meyer store. His father pulled the cycle into a gas station. "Limp in, leap out, at Leapy Lind's," the sign said. Leapy came out to the pump and shoved the nozzle into the opening near Chris's leg. He pumped the big handle beside the gas pump and Chris saw the red gasoline rise in the clear container at the top; he stopped at two gallons and then opened the nozzle. The strong odor of gasoline filled the air.

His father pulled a handful of change out of his pocket, and as he sorted the coins, he said, "Say Leapy, you seen Speed?"

"Nope," said Leapy, hanging up the nozzle. "He owe you?"

"Well, sure, who doesn't he owe?" his father said, laughing. "Says he'd rather owe you than beat you out of it. But we was supposed to go sickle riding last week and he never showed."

"Aw," Leapy said, taking the coins. "Speed's a guy you can't keep track of." They drove across the street and parked in front of Ptomaine Tommy's, a railroad car converted to a single counter cafe. Inside, in the airless heat of the train car, a fly buzzed against the fly paper which hung from a light cord; the sticky yellow paper was melting like wax.

"Hiya, Howard, Howya doing?"

"Ya want the lunch?" Mable asked.

"Naw, we ain't very hungry," his father said, counting his change. "Why, believe I'll have java and sinkers. Give the squirt some ice cream."

Chris looked up from the punchboard he had been reading and said "I'd like a vanilla cone."

The lazy swaap-swaap of the overhead fan, the buzz of the mixer, the fly fighting against the sticky paper, the small juke box, the stool that rotated against his seat all made him happy. His mother would never have stopped in a place like Ptomaine Tommy's; she would never say things like java or mocha or a cup of mud and sinkers or wet your whistle. He liked to hear the truckers joking, talking about Manchuria, the price of gas, how long it took to get to Frisco on 101.

"We'll get that joint," his father said, "don't you worry. We'll be home for lunch."

His father's optimism and the ice cream, cold and creamy against the edges of his tongue, cheered him. He hoped that they would find the part and he looked forward to sitting in the warm sun of his own yard, resting against the Hudson's high tire while his father worked on the car. Those were the Saturdays he loved, the day steeped in the pungent odor of warm rubber and oil and sunbaked enamel.

"Where you working, Howard?" asked Tommy.

His father dunked the doughnut, slurped the coffee noisily, poured what was in the saucer back into the cup, and asked for a refill. "Got a job Monday on the Columbia," he said, blowing on the cup to cool it, "if I get there." He dunked the doughnut, winked at Chris, his mouth full. "I'll be on easy street, no more bread and relief gravy."

"Is that WPA?" asked Tommy.

"Hell no, ain't you heard? That's Corps of Army Engineers—big project. That's no tree-planting make-work project." The truck drivers had stopped talking and were looking at his father who was now rolling a cigarette. His tongue moved quickly along the edge of the paper and it was in his mouth, lit and he was puffing furiously on it. "That's a big job," he said, so softly that Tommy could not have heard him. Then he laid some coins on the counter, hitched up his pants, and motioned toward the door.

"See ya, Tommy, Mable."

Outside heat rolled off the street in waves, and the cycle flooded; his father swore as his high-laced logging boot fell again and again until the cycle backfired, caught, pumped blue smoke raggedly into the air. "C'mon, let's go and see if we can get that part from a white man."

They went north on 82nd, and when the air against his face grew cooler, Chris knew that they were catching the wind from the Columbia. They stopped at Easy Jack's, bouncing over the rutted entrance and pulling up to the shack. Jack was on a chair just inside the doorway, a beer in his hand, listening to the ball game from Beaver Stadium. He waved a fat hand.

"Hiya, Jack. I need a U-joint for a '30 Hudson 8," his father said, looking around the yard. Jack never took anything off a car until it could be sold, so there were no bins of parts; the rusting hulks were whatever parts they contained, and if the customer took the parts off he saved ten per cent (in which case, his father had said, the price was jacked up by twenty per cent).

"Betcha. Got a '30 Hudson over in the corner."

"You don't mind if I go into your yard, do you?" his father said with mock politeness. "You're not like the hebe down the street?" Easy Jack's laugh followed them as they went into the yard, past cars bursting with blackberry vines and high grass. Hornets and bees dotted the sky above wrecks, and their hum was like a high-pitched engine. The Hudson against the fence was, like theirs, a foot taller than his father and its blue paint, almost hidden under the rain-streaked dust, was shifting through rainbow patterns to a strange purple. His father dropped to the ground, parted the grass, and said: "Nerts."

He sat on the warped runningboard and for a second Chris saw worry in his eyes. He had figured to be home by now, to have the Hudson repaired and washed and gassed and ready for Monday.

Slowly he got up and Chris followed him to the shack. "She ain't there, the whole driveshaft is gone."

"Yar? Guess I sold it," Easy Jack said. "Well, if Abe and Swede don't have it the next bet would be the Gyp."

"The Gyp's a big a crook as Abe. I'll buy my parts from a white man. And that's almost to Vancouver," he said, spitting, looking at his pocket watch and then at the sky. "But dammit, we're halfway now. Listen I can't take the squirt all the way on the sickle. Let me borrow a car and I'll leave the sickle here."

Easy Jack tipped forward and looked at the cycle, as if estimating its value, then at the row of cars that faced the street. "Okay, that there Model A tudor is a sweet runner."

"Thanks, Jack, that's white of you." he said, grabbing Chris' hand. The sedan was black with red wire wheels, when Chris opened his door hot air rushed out, and they quickly rolled down the windows and cranked the windshield open. His father lifted the hood and opened the petcock; he kicked the starter button but the battery was dead. "Here's what none of these new cars got," he said, taking a crank from under the seat, he turned on the ignition and set the choke and spark levers. He disappeared beyond the radiator and then Chris saw him spring up, the engine caught, churned in brief erratic spurts until his father ran around the fender to alter the spark and choke. "Whew! Sometimes she'll start, sometimes break your arm."

Chris squirmed against the hot ragged mohair, but he liked the feel of the car. They sat high, the breeze from beneath the windshield fanned them dissipating the oil smoke and heat which came through the firewall. Chris liked the sound of the engine which staggered perkily through the gears.

"Sweet little engine, except for the babbit rods. I had a couple of these back home."

"And you built a snowbuggy out of one." Chris said.

"But give me a V-8 anyday. Give me something with sass."

They drove down 82nd to Columbia Boulevard and turned left, heading toward North Portland. Beside them the Columbia flowed, a grand expanse of water, and beyond it he could see Mt. St. Helens glowing white against the clear blue sky.

"When I get this job, first thing I'm going to buy you is a B-B gun and that's a promise. That job'll likely last a year, maybe two, and we'll get your mother a refrigerator. Maybe we'll get a new car." His father dreamed through the yellowed glass of the windshield, and Chris prayed that he would get the part and the job. With a refrigerator they could put Kool-aid in the trays with toothpicks like Buzz's mother did to make popsicles. His mother would like that too. She wanted things to be nice, had planted hen and chickens in hot water tanks and had pots of geraniums along the old wooden front porch; she had made curtains for every window. She tried to fix up their house, and therefore, she hated the old cars that his father hauled home to park in the driveway and in the front yard—making it look like a minor junk yard—and she was ashamed of what the neighbors must think. She would like it if they got a new car.

Chris dreamed as they drove through the sleepy, hot afternoon; he liked to talk with his father, to hear his voice, smell his tobacco, oil, sweat, and he thought that they were like two people on a comfortable island moving through time. When he grew up he wanted to know everything his father knew—how to build a house, do wiring, plumbing, overhaul an engine—but most of all he wanted to be able like his father, to drive or run or fly anything.

The car turned right on Union Avenue, toward Jantzen Beach Park, and just as Chris could see the top of the roller-coaster structure above the trees his father pulled into the Gyp's yard. Over the board fence the rows of roof-tops glowed, the bright eyes of windshields, proof of a thousand mistakes. The sign said Milt's Auto Parts, but beside the front door were battered refrigerators and stoves, phonographs, magazines and books, tricycles, scooters, racks of used clothing. Inside Chris was struck by the darkness and the odor of mildew and terrible food. The counter was on the left, and a davenport with stained lace doilies was on the right; it held a huge woman in bright clothes, and two small naked children played at her feet.

9

Chris heard his father ask the man for the part but his attention was held by the woman who picked up a child and bounced it on her knee–the wide-loop earrings shaking, rings flashing, the bright green blouse and orange skirt catching the dim light.

"Come," she said to him. "I bless your money."

He looked at his feet, heard his father say; "Be glad to take it off myself, if necessary."

"I bless your money," she said. "Tell your fortune."

"Oh go ahead, Chris. Here," he said, flipping him a nickel which he missed. It hit the wall, rolled across the floor and she was off the couch, scooping it into her hand. "I bless," she said, rubbing the nickel against the crotch of her dress. She was laughing and his father was laughing. "You're going to be lucky, Chris."

"Would you like to see the dance?" she said, motioning to a door. "My three beautiful daughters will dance for you."

His father was in a good mood and when he reached into his shirt pocket Chris thought he was getting a dollar but his hand came out with the makings. "Uh not today," he said, smiling. As the match flared the man came back rubbing his hands to say that he didn't have the part, new or used.

They sat in the car for a few minutes while his father smoked the cigarette. The woman had not brought them luck, they had thrown away a nickel. Chris, irritated by all this delay, began to ask why they didn't just go back to Swede's A-1 Parts and buy the new U-joint, and then he somehow realized that his father did not have the money for a new joint. All the talk about new cars and refrigerators was just talk, and in fact his father didn't have the money to repair a twenty dollar Hudson.

Chris felt despair and frustration but his father's mood picked up almost immediately. "Well, squirt," he said, starting the car off the battery and heading back for Easy Jack's. "this sure ain't our day, is it?" In the distance, Mt. Hood danced against a pure blue sky. "Those gypsies usually live in old stores," his father said, "You see them along Burnside and skid row. Some say they steal babies." His father talked on, amused by the world and curious about all that happened around him; he beat out a rhythm on the steering wheel, began to whistle an aimless melody, then said: "There are sure lots of funny people in this world."

With more impatience in his voice than he had intended, Chris said, "Why don't you trade the sickle for this car?"

"Um could. Hate to get rid of it though. Could ride the sickle there if I put on a headlight and mufflers. What I should do is fix the Hudson, trade it for another car." Chris could see that the wheels in his father's head were turning, trying to salvage all this directionless driving. "Except I'd like to get something, you know, better. Maybe a Packard or a Buick, people notice a man driving them. Maybe I could trade the Hudson and the sickle for something better, and then eventually use that as a down payment on a new car. I sure like those new Lincolns," he said, dreaming, his thoughts as distant as the mountains which shimmered above the ridged horizon, and then he hit the brakes hard, slowing them and finally stopping them beside the road when a rear wheel locked.

Chris looked around, startled, and his father said: "Hitchhiker." He always stopped for hitchhikers because he had been on the bum, although his mother said that was a good way to get killed. The door was jerked open and his seat pushed forward as the person got in back, and before Chris could see who it was he smelled dead fish, sweat, a hot stickly odor that made his stomach churn. The car moved on the road again and Chris turned to the back seat; the man was an Indian.

"How far you going, buddy?"

"Celilo," he said. When he leaned forward Chris smelled tobacco and whiskey, the sour odor of onions. "Going home."

"That's a long ways, but you got a good day for it. We're turning at 82nd but you ought to get another ride easy."

Oil smoke mixed with the rancid odor from the backseat and Chris shifted uneasily toward the thin stream of air that came from under the windshield.

"Say, how's fishing up there?" his father asked. "You guys get some good cut-throat?"

Once they had driven along the Columbia beyond The Dalles, leaving Portland at dawn and around noon they had passed the shanties of Celilo Falls, the Indian fishing rounds—tiny houses made of tin and cardboard and plywood, and at the edge of the river a rough scaffolding of timbers from which the Indians fished. It was a beautiful place but, his father said, the Indians sure didn't know how to take care of it.

The Indian didn't answer; his father said, "I'll be working near there-at the big dam they're building. You know where I mean?"

"Ruining the river,' the Indian said. "Soon no fish. I gotta get home."

The stop light at 82nd Street grew closer and his father slowed to let the Indian out. "Keep going. I got to get home."

The car slowed and then picked up speed to continue across the intersection.

Chris smelled the strong breath and turning slightly, he saw the knife point held at his father's neck: "I'm a crazy Indian." Chris froze, saw from the edge of his eye the dark hand with black hairs along the back, the thick blunt fingers which held the wide ragged blade, the profile of the swarthy, pock-marked face. His father gripped the wheel and looked straight ahead, the knife point forming a slight indentation beside the large vein. A sign drifted past: Columbia River Boulevard became Highway 30 and ahead was Troudale, Hood River, and far beyond, maybe a hundred miles, where the river grew narrow between the basalt cliffs was Celilo.

They drove in silence, the shadows already beginning to flatten, and soon the knife disappeared; the Indian sat back and sighed deeply, as if he was exhausted by simply driving. Chris suddenly found himself less worried about their being found murdered beside the road, and more concerned about the rumbling in his stomach. He dreamed of home, the cool shade of his back yard where he could be right now eating peanut butter sandwiches and reading comic books. When he left home, he had thought he would be right back, and now it looked as though he would be in Celilo tonight, hungry, fighting the cold desert wind.

12

The knife away from his throat, his father finally spoke. "Cripe, mister, we can't go all that way. Have a heart."

"Drive," he said. "Got anything to eat?"

"God, I wish we did. Wish I had something to wet my whistle, even if it was some good old Bull Run. Tell me, the cops after you?"

Chris looked down the road for a roadblock but there was only the smooth unbroken asphalt. The river below was a mirror, reflecting a white sailboat and a cloudless sky. To the right, Troutdale was a few houses under the sharp pine and fir trees.

"Look, lemme stop for gas."

"Keep driving," he said, leaning forward, bringing the stench of sour food and sweat to Chris. The knife in his hand rested on the back of the seat cushion.

"Okee, mister, but don't blame me. By the way, what're you wanted for?" The road narrowed and began to climb; Crown Point was a dark mass, a gigantic head. The air grew cooler; against the mountains there was no sunlight, and when they went through a tunnel carved out of solid basalt the darkness was like night. From this height, he knew the fear of falling; only the quad rail of hand-fitted rock, a WPA job that his father had helped with, kept them from the river far below.

"Did you kill somebody?"

"Huh, he said. "Looking for work at the hiring hall. Sonofabitch I slept under the Burnside Bridge—all night long the cars went over. All that money."

"That's all? Shoot, that's nothing. Why I thought...." His father suddenly relaxed, one hand falling to the seat; then Chris noticed that he had been fishing for the crank with his foot, and now his hand edged toward it.

"They ask my social security number—who the hell's got one? I'll tell you," he said, swaying as the car caught a gust of wind from the river, "I'm a crazy Indian and mad enough to kill."

They rounded a curve and far ahead he saw the scenic turnout. As they neared the wide place, his father got the crank into his lap and held it tightly with one hand, while the Indian raved about Roosevelt; at that moment, as Chris reached for the

13

door handle ready to jump, the engine faltered, the car bucked, ran for a few seconds, lurched again, and that was all. His father released the crank and said, almost with relief, "That's it—she's out of gas." He coasted into the turnout and braked, the front wheels coming to rest against the stone embankment a few hundred feet above the river. An osprey hovered at their eye level, a speck in the wind currents.

Because he didn't know what else to do, Chris opened the door to stand in the chilly wind that swept up from the river; the Indian squeezed past, walking silently if unsteadily across the road. He followed it without looking back.

"Up shit creek without a paddle," his father said, pushing his cap back. "He would have stabbed me, that crazy mutt—they oughta keep them all on the reservation. I never seen an Indian who could drink like a white man."

Chris was colder and hungrier than he had ever been and he was scared; he had to keep his chin from shaking to speak. "What'll we do?"

"That crazy bastard," his father said, kneeling on the front seat and lifting up the rear cushion; he took out a length of red rubber hose. "Maybe the trunk," he said, getting out, going to the metal box at the rear of the car; he came back with a gas can.

"Empty," he said.

They looked both ways along the road; the Indian was out of sight. "Could hoof it back to Troutdale, maybe get a ride. Lemme think." He got his tobacco and paper and rolled a cigarette. Chris realized that his father would hitchhike into Troutdale but he knew Chris couldn't keep up, not in that cold wind and he wouldn't leave him alone.

"What it musta been like," his father said, gesturing with his cigarette out the yellowed windshield at the river and the basalt cliffs on the Washington side.

"What it musta been like before the roads, before the loggers." His father began to muse about the beauties of the country, about how glad he was that he had moved to Oregon, about the freedom and room and possibilities that the country held. Time stopped by his father's talk, and in spite of the goose pimples on his arms and the gnawing hunger that filled his stomach, Chris dozed off and as the wind from the gorge rocked the car gently back and forth he fell asleep.

He awoke later to a concussion, the sound of a door slamming. The sky had grown dark and thunderheads swelled from the Cascades, their lower edges becoming a white mist which rolled toward the river. He turned, confused from sleep, and saw that another car had stopped at the viewpoint; his father moved toward it in quick steps, the gas can in his hand. He gestured toward their sedan and finally the man rolled down his window a few inches–they no doubt thought his father was some nut waiting to do them harm on this desolate road. The car was large, dark green, and expensive looking. When the man got out Chris was surprised to see he was a Negro who towered over his father. He unlocked the gas cap and waited beside the fender while his father bent down, put one end of the hose into the tank and the other into his mouth, then quickly tipped it into the can. In a few minutes he was up, folding the hose, and reaching into his pocket for money which the tall Negro refused. He hurried back and through the windshield Chris saw him smile; he opened the cowl cap, carefully poured in the gallon of gas, threw the can and hose in the trunk and got in.

"Well, squirt, we're on our way," he said, slapping Chris on the leg. The engine turned, caught, and they headed back toward Portland; not until they entered the first tunnel did his father speak again. "Rich bitches. Moneybags. Wonder where that buck got the car?"

They drove and it seemed to Chris that they had been driving forever, mile after mile around in a big circle, and they did not have the part. They were no better off than they had been this morning.

The rain caught them near Troutdale–a river storm, the huge drops sweeping across the road in a solid sheet, entering the car at every crack. The windshield wiper didn't work so his father had to drive with one hand and work the little lever on the wiper blade with the other. He drove slowly, his face close to the glass.

"Oregon mist," his father joked. "Mist California and hit Oregon."

As the storm enveloped them, the sky ahead grew blacker, and the car seemed to go more slowly—finally it was inching along, moving at a snail's pace into the night, and Chris closed his eyes, afraid that they might drive forever without getting anywhere they wanted to be, or worse, that they might run out of gas again on this dismal narrow road or fall into the dark waters below. His bare feet were numb with cold; he began to shake.

Years later he would remember the darkness of that moment, the howl of wind and rain, the lightning that arced in long white flashes from somewhere above Mt. Hood all the way to their radiator cap it seemed, and wonder what his father was thinking. Did he have fears? Did he know despair, that churning nausea in the lower stomach that takes the breath away, the sense of emptiness—or had his daily failures come to be an insulation against the bigger forms of failure? Did he worry about death, already treading upon his heels?

"Hey. There's a good junkyard outside Gresham."

The optimism of those words, the eternal hopefulness! They inched through the blackness, their dim headlights could barely probe, through a deluge such as Chris had never known. The wind driving water through every tiny crack in the floor, windows, windshield, doors, pouring over his bare feet, and yet his father looked for the blue sky, the rainbow which hovered somewhere slightly beyond human sight.

Somehow they got to Troutdale; where the yellow lights within cozy houses seemed to taunt them, and his father turned south, the Model A groaning upgrade from the river to the foothills of the Cascades. In the forest it was darker, wetter, more lonesome.

"Boy, oh boy. Jack's gonna wonder where his car went."

They emerged from the forest and the land leveled into small neat farms and in the distance Gresham was a patch of lights sparkling against the raindrops on the windshield. The sky lightened as the storm clouds passed to the west, but immediately, before any rainbow could appear, the true darkness of night enveloped them. The junkyard was a city block off the main road and they bounced along the ruts, his father swearing at every chuck hole. There were no lights except for the small naked bulb beside a battered trailer house; it illuminated the warped plywood of the trailer and a cloud of insects that fluttered wildly against the margins of the night.

"Stay here." His father slammed the door and sprinted across the muddy apron, his shirt growing dark with rain drops as he shook the door handle. Chris waited, as his father entered the dark building he thought how much he liked Sundays–toast and milk-coffee and oatmeal, the colored funnies. If company was coming there might be roast beef and dark gravy, or meatloaf, and Perfection salad, his favorite. The house would be warm and friendly, filled with talk. Sometimes they went to the movies and in the evening, curled into a cozy pillow, he liked to listen to the radio.

He was still dreaming of this perfect day when his father came back, his clothes soaking wet, hands greasy, the skin of one knuckle a bloody flap; he smiled, held up the rusty joint. "Got it," he said, starting the car; his voice carried a note of triumph but Chris saw that he was shivering. "Cost four-bits–I couldn't jew the bastard down."

His father had the universal joint, he would get it on the Hudson, perhaps get the job, and they would, Chris hoped, be on easy street. But it was fulfillment tinged with despair as open fields became farms, became yards and he tried to see into the windows of each house, wondering about the lives that passed behind curtains. Streets grew familiar and soon he was back in his own neighborhood, where he knew every bush, field, tree, hole.

"I'll let you off." his father said. "And get the sickle. Here, take this." Chris took the rusted universal joint and then he was home, climbing stiffly from the floor to running-board to his own yard. He put the joint on the floor of the Hudson and went into the house.

His mother was ironing in the kitchen. "Where the devil have you guys been?" she asked.

17

"We got the car part." he said, leaning against the cupboard, feeling very tired. The house felt so warm and comfortable; there was a large kettle of soup cooking, and in the front room his sister was listening to the radio. He tried to tell her where they had been but he kept thinking about his bed and peanut butter sandwiches and the radio. "And Mom, there was this Indian."

She told him to get into some dry clothes; he went into the room he and his sister shared, moving with extreme slowness, but when he put on clean clothes he felt better. He heard the roar of the Harley coming down the street and went to the front room window; in the half-light he saw his father shake the water from his hands–he was soaked from the ride home–and open the door of the Hudson. He got the universal joint from the car and climbed under it, working by flashlight. From the warm house Chris watched drops falling from the eaves and he saw his father lying on the wet ground, feet dug in to push himself farther under the car until all he could see were the soles of his boots. As Chris watched he wondered if there was any way to win–in some ways his father was the smartest man in the world, and yet he would always be broke, he would always be replacing the broken parts with worn parts, trying to shave a price and hoping somehow to come out slightly ahead. Chris watched the sheets of water running down the sides of the Hudson, saw the boots struggling beneath the car–he knew that next Saturday that joint or something else would need to be replaced, and by tomorrow morning a thin coat of rust would be forming on the tools that his father would have left on the lawn.

Memory: Returning To An Empty Intersection

Boy and bike heel through dawn
Down smooth walks, and bearings
Turn easy: there is no friction.
Underwheel the shopmen tidy up;
Their water dissipates into mist
And memory. Like the handlebar
Foxtail tossing gently back in
The wind. the boy's hair is thick,
Eyes sharp. lungs clear: life
Is easywheeling with good bearings.

Down smooth cement and a tailwind.
On the fountain counter he sees
Glasses stand like all his days:
Full and empty. some with straws.

Lents: Early Sunday Morning

The sun angled across the grey sidewalk and black asphalt; the shadows were cool, plum-grey. The flat brilliant light emphasized textures: stucco and terracotta, tiled facades and angled drain pipes, bricks beneath concrete, the sidewalks age, garbage cans, the streets like vacant fields, the empty mouth of an alley.

No building was taller than a telephone pole: Rexall and Mt. Scott drugs, Stella's variety, Menashe's, Butterfield's grocery, Eggiman's meat market, Harold's cafe. All had their awnings drawn; the endless spiral of Bud's barber pole was still. Missing letters on the Aero's marquee spelled what was not playing: the litter, the cold popcorn, the urinal's trickle. The fire hydrant's shadow was a long dog. Near the curb a newspaper threatened to move.

Second story rooms sent messages with the semaphore of shades. Here was the mystery: who would live over Reilly's tavern, the Rose Lantern, where the echoes of juke boxes and laughter were like fallen bones? Sauerkraut and sausage, tobacco smoke, stale beer, dustballs, wooden matches wedged in floor cracks. Like the Goodwill and second-hand stores these rooms displayed the dumb evidence of other lives. In time slippers would shuffle down dark hallways toward the bathroom, the coffee would perk, radio play Baptist music—a wracking cough, pipes rattling in walls, silverware clattering in the afternoons of memory. A faded wash dress would dance on the line between two chimneys, celebrating life.

But now the air was cool, brittle, slightly metallic, like stone or spice, and defined all with the clarity of a dream: this space, that structure, this place. The air continued upward. The sky was blue, unbroken by clouds, birds, smoke. One star was still visible directly overhead, growing dim.

Corner of
92nd and Foster
Lents, Oregon

Courtesy of the
Oregon Historical
Society

Sunday Night

Walking in the rain of the unloved,
the darkness between arc lights
an unreasonable distance.
The isolated glow of houses
like ships passing, and I knew,
somehow, every house was empty.
Who could survive such melancholy?

Trudging toward Lents, dim neon,
and like a man stepping off a cliff
I could not consider Monday.

There is no rain as endless as Oregon.

The 'Thirties as Allegory

I watch the late-late show
only for cars: I trust the traffic
of high roofs and clamshell fenders.
Craftsmen cared, and their product
seems indestructible. Built of real steel
these autos survive silly accidents; one feels
somehow they could never deal death.

This is reflected in the plot I don't watch:
in black and white conflicts are resolved;
the bad guys go to jail, or ache their blood
in gutters under virtue's heel. Off-stage,
the boy really does get the girl.

Dazed by sound, the verisimilitude of screen,
the audience stumbles sleepily on popcorn
into unpolluted air. They climb up
into their car, from curb to running-board
to floor to seat—into the pure smell of leather
and enamel, gas and oil—and roll on high tires
over empty streets toward an uncomplicated house,
where an ice-box thrives on ice.

                          Their bed
is simple, flat, square as their yard
where no intruder travels; in sleep
the subliminal film unreels, blots out dark
streamlined clouds of War.

The Chicken Which Became a Rat

"He ain't *eating* the eggs," Uncle Boswick said. His voice carried that same amazed indignation as when he had asked my father, "Yer *paid* for the window?" or when he had reported to me, "He did it with the *sam-yer-eye*." His world had its own practical logic, of survival; these were acts which left him confounded. "The Jap ain't eating the eggs and he won't sell them."

"What's he plan to do?" I asked.

"No plans." Uncle Boswick shook the beads of dew from his slacks and pointed his whangee cane across the tall grass which stretched from our house to the Jap's tarpaper shack: within the wire I could imagine the gaunt. long-necked hens eyeing each other suspiciously. "Nothing—the chickens are getting wild, the eggs are piling up, the garden's full of weeds—I don't get it."

And then, after picking out the grass kernels which jutted from his perforated two-tone shoes, Uncle Boswick was off to the USO club. To build the boys' morale.

I was surprised that his attitude toward the Jap had changed from hatred to an amazed indignation. The Jap had disappointed him. Eggs were rationed and Uncle Boswick saw the Jap's reluctance to sell his not as a foreign plot but rather as evidence of the humorless intensity of a backward race: Uncle Boswick would know how to make money here, somehow, if the Jap would only work with him.

What surprised me most was the change in the Jap's property: weeds choked the garden, the corn stalks were stunted and brown, the chicken coop was a box of rusty wire, a small concentration camp. If Uncle Boswick was baffled, how could I be expected to understand? But it seemed that after V-E Day the Jap had given up, as if he knew the Allies would win, and now the land was reverting to the desolation it had been a year ago—a wasteland beyond the city's limits, marshy in winter, baked hard in summer. It now resembled the useless landscape of before last spring, when one night the Jap had infiltrated our neighborhood.

He had sneaked in without noise or luggage, and the next morning, when I peeked through the gun-slot of venetian blinds, he was on the flatlands, bent to his hoe, against the rising sun.

It was the third year of the War.

His blade flashed like a bayonet into American soil. Silhouetted against the sun which spilled red across the tips of furrows, his insect shape reminded me of something I had seen or read–something thin, creepy, and utterly evil.

Then I recalled the source. On the coffee table was the current issue of *Liberty*: on the cover Hitler assumed the body of a jackass, his hoofs kicking Europe; beside him Mussolini was a baboon, dangling mindlessly from a war-wrecked tree; and in the upper-right corner Tojo was a furry, menacing spider whose web, like the land around our Jap, was stained blood-red.

The pavement ended at our house and Home Front defenses honey-combed the neighborhood's perimeter. The day after the sneak attack on Pearl Harbor we had marched into this wasteland and each boy had dug a foxhole, a hiding place against the bombing raids which seemed imminent. The only bombs to fall were random fire balloons which fizzled out in the wet forests west of Portland: but as weeks turned to months into years, all our young muscle was directed at the War Effort. We dug a gridwork of slit trenches, pillboxes, and tunnels, and for armament we had stacks of dirt clods, stones, bags of smoke dust, apples drilled to accept a firecracker, and of course our B-B guns. Uncle Boswick had often said that we could expect a Presidential E. flag.

Into these trenches we crawled – Piggy, Slats, Mike, The MacGregor, and myself–soot streaked across our faces, like Commandos in movies; and we moved out, sinking low until the last observation post, where smooth throwing rocks and solid dirt clods were piled. For we were children of war, and had been taught to hate.

"I can smell him," The MacGregor said.

I crawled to the rim and partly turned, one eye on the Jap and the other on The MacGregor, who braced a foot against the dirt wall, his arm cocked. When I raised my finger he fired a distance round. It sailed across the broken landscape and dropped so far behind the Jap did not pause in his stroke.

"Correct elevation." I whispered.

The MacGregor sent off another stone, which arced white against the blue, until falling, it became a black speck lost in the weeds. Still the enemy hoed on.

I realized that if The MacGregor, our strongest gunner, couldn't make the distance, none of us could. But I whispered. "Harassment rounds," and raised two fingers, which meant fire at will.

Our hate spun five clods upward, where they teetered against the sky, to fall in uneven arcs on the dull ground. The Jap, untouched, continued his insidious ground work, chopping treacherously at this piece of the United States, knocking crystals of dew from the weeds as he enlarged his claim.

Over our heads a whistle pierced the sky.

The black speck seemed to travel forever in its swift, guided flight, diminishing until it reached an invisible peak; with a flash of white, the gesture of a wingtip, it peeled off, screaming earthward, to crash through the window of the Jap's shanty. The enemy jumped, dropped his hoe, and ran, flapping his wings like a chicken attempting flight.

We cheered, and as I turned to see who our supporting artillery might be, a volley of laughter strafed the field. At the edge of the pavement Uncle Boswick flipped a heavy stone from hand to hand; he looked more than ever like the posters of Uncle Sam.

It was toward the Jap that he pointed: I want you.

I could not understand why my father, when he learned of our victory, carefully folded the evening paper, hitched up his pants and strode down the street, off the pavement and across the field.

He was gone a long time, and dinner was halfway through before he returned. In fact, Uncle Boswick was well into seconds, his mouth so full he could barely exclaim: "Yer *paid* for the window?"

29

"But why?" I asked. Was he a traitor? Aiding the enemy. I almost believed this in spite of the signs on our front door glass: We Bought Our Quota. We Have A Boy in the NAVY; the blue cloth with the gold star. V for Victory...

"Because your Uncle broke it." he said, spreading white margarine on his bread, digging into the Relief gravy over cereal-laden hamburger. "And because what that Jap does on that gawdforsaken land is none of your business."

Now I could not believe it. I felt sick, confused, as shattered as the Jap's window. I looked to Uncle Boswick, but he was smiling as he snubbed out his cigarette–smoked as usual to the middle. Another wasteful habit which aggravated my mother.

"Just leave him alone," my father said quietly, always chewing. "Stay away from his place."

Uncle Boswick could not tolerate the sight of my father calmly eating supper, asking us to leave the Jap alone. "But he's the ENEMY!" he shouted, fists clenched on the table.

"How do you know?" my father asked.

"Well... he'sa gawdamn Jap. ain't he?"

"There," I said, jumping up. pointing to the wall. "There." On the kitchen wall were two pages my mother had torn from *Life* magazine: "How to Tell Japs From the Chinese." The photos had an overlay to show that Chinese have long, fine-boned faces, parchment yellow complexion, and never have rosy cheeks; Japs have squat faces with the nose a flat blob, earthy yellow complexion, and sometimes rosy cheeks. I read: "An often sounder clue is facial expression, shaped by cultural not anthropological factors. Chinese wear rational calm of tolerant realists. Japs, like General Tojo, show humorless intensity of ruthless mystics." The other page showed Tall Chinese brothers and Short Japanese admirals–our allies and our enemies.

"He looked just like the Short Japanese admirals, and..."

"Did he have rosy cheeks?" my father asked, smiling.

"Yes," I said, although I really wasn't sure. I hadn't been able to see my enemy's face.

"I don't like that Jap any better than you do," my father said, looking at me, Uncle Boswick, and my mother, "But he's had a rough row to hoe." As he cleaned his plate with a final slice of bread, he repeated the story the Jap had told him: there had been a large farm near Gresham, where the fields sloped off toward the sun, and where seeds would not stay in the ground—in spring the strawberries grew big as a boy's fist, and in fall the corn was so large and tender that a single ear would make a meal. My father told the story in the dreamy, tragic tone of a man who has not owned anything himself—saying that in only two more years the farm would have been paid off, but after Pearl Harbor it was confiscated by the government and sold at auction, and the Jap—a Nisei, who had been born on the farm, and was therefore an American citizen—had spent the past two and a half years in an internment camp near Pendleton. Now released, he had no family, no farm, no money. "So I think you—everybody—ought to lay off him."

"Whadda think the Nips're doing to our boys?" Uncle Boswick shouted. "Wake Island, Bataan, the Death March. And don't forget Pearl Harbor: those jokers didn't pay us for any broken windows there. I wish..."

My mother got up and began to clear the table. No doubt she was thinking of Grant on the USS Plymouth, now a month out of Hawaii. My father rolled Bugler into tan, wheat-straw paper, touched his tongue to the edge and flattened the ends. He always enjoyed one of Uncle Boswick's real cigarettes after dinner, but he would not ask; nor was one offered tonight.

The last thing I heard as I got up and went to sit on the front porch was Uncle Boswick finishing his sentence: "...I could get my licks in."

Uncle Boswick was our hero. The Declaration of War was being read over a million radio speakers when Uncle Boswick's foot missed a tailgate at Fort Ord; he lay screaming in pain as Roosevelt's voice called for unlimited sacrifices from our fighting men. The truck had been barely moving, but something had happened to Uncle Boswick's back. He was given a medical discharge and a fifty per cent disability pension, which meant he did not need to work even if he could. In the confusion of that December the papers officially honoring him as the first casualty of the war were lost in channels, but Uncle Boswick got the pension, a Purple Heart, and freedom from rationing: he had unlimited supplies at the airbase PX. It was unfortunate, my mother often said, that the PX did not stock eggs and meat, but only cigarettes and liquor.

With my father it was different: he was 4-F.

At times I felt that he was letting us down by not being in uniform. Oh sure, building Liberty Ships was pretty important work, but I could not get too excited about it—not even on those days when we would go to Swan Island for a launching, when after the speeches and free lunch he would show us the whirly crane he drove, a tiny cab sitting a hundred feet high on delicate girder legs. But seeing it sail down the tracks, with a bulkhead dangling from the long cables, just wasn't the same as seeing those thin, censored V-letters that The MacGregor's father sent from North Africa.

So I could not understand why he had paid for the Jap's window. Although we were not so poor as we had been before the war, there was no money to spend foolishly. Oh, perhaps I had a vague idea why my father had paid off: because he believed that every man should own a piece of ground and a house, and that all others should respect the limits of ownership—even if it was a house no better than ours, where the wind whipped through the ivy-covered lattice-work which was its foundation.

As I looked through dusk across the field I could see the Jap, his hoe flashing in the dim light. The sight made me furious. How were we to leave him alone? He was the enemy: newspapers, magazines, our teachers, had taught us to hate him. And we learned well to hate. Oh, how we hated him—deeply, intensely. He was the grinning monkey-pilot who gleefully leaned into his gunsight to machinegun parachutists. He was the spidery Nip who saved bullets by using his bayonet on the wounded. We knew too well of his exquisite tortures—bamboo splinters ignited under toenails, fingernails removed by pliers, the eye-lid lifted off by the knife's thin whisper.

These thoughts were bothering me when Uncle Boswick came out to sit on the porch, "What I'd like to know is how he got *released*. With a War on."

"Maybe he escaped," I suggested.

"He's up to something," Uncle Boswick whispered.' "Keep your eye on him, kid. That slant-eyed devil is a spy or a saboteur."

Our eyes were on him all right. Every day after breakfast Piggy, Slats, Mike, The MacGregor, and I gathered in the farthest observation post. We pushed Uncle Boswick's binoculars over the rim of the hole until the lenses were full of yellow skin— earthy yellow, I was sure. We harassed the Jap with random shots. We saluted him with raised middle-fingers and screamed Banzai, and asked how the hell Tojo was.

But the Jap refused to notice us, and anyway, we saw nothing suspicious. Just the hoe striking the ground and weeds flung from the tiny green shoots which were beginning to appear. This went on for a week, and suddenly the eighth day was Summer. By ten o'clock it was seventy, the flatlands shimmered, and the Jap, slashing with his hoe or carrying buckets of water, looked like a movie mirage.

The OP was an oven. When Piggy refused to drink brackish canteen water, he went home. Then Mike remembered the bandoliers of ice in his mother's refrigerator. Soon only The MacGregor and myself sweated in the hole, pouring water over our heads, swearing, hating the Jap for keeping us there.

And at noon, when the sun was straight up, erasing any shade, we went swimming.

But the War, glorious and dreadful, near and distant, continued to touch us in many ways. Every day my mother scanned the paper fearfully:

TODAY'S ARMY-NAVY CASUALTY LIST

Washington-Following are the latest casualties in the military services, including next of kin.

ARMY-NAVY DEAD

Her finger would tremble through the list to where Grant's last name, first name, rank, might be; then the newspaper would collapse in her folded hands and she would cry or pray or both. Sometimes, in the afternoon when the house was empty, I would burst in from play to find her at the writing desk, sobbing over a stack of tissue-thin V-letters; they were all postmarked San Francisco's Censor's Office, and she was wondering, no doubt, where in the wide Pacific her oldest .boy might be.

Elsewhere, Captain America turned bullets off his shield, the Green Lantern sought truth, and even the Submariner turned to the side of good: another ring of filthy rotten Nazi spies and saboteurs was broken. The Axis shed their animal skins in defeat. In our comics we fought the war, and in the papers we read of its progress: June 6th was D-Day; during that month V-1 bombs, a terrible undreamed of weapon, began to fall on England; the Marianas Campaign pushed ahead. The pleasant summer advanced, and so did our boys: troops landed at Saipan, and during July the big drive began through Normandy; Guam and Paris were liberated in August.

At home the war controlled us. Our battles were fought every day: we could buy comic books, but few fireworks and no bubblegum. The B-B's for our guns turned to lead. The currency of conversation was ration discs and coupon books. In our driveway my father's 1934 Terraplane sat without tires, graded by the C sticker on its windshield. Now he drove only the sedan, a 1930 Hudson. It was an immense, magnificent car, dark and square; and when he placed an ironing board across the jump seats he was able to haul nine people every day to the ship-yard. However essential this was to the war effort, he could not get the red and white B sticker changed to the coveted grade A—so the coupe rested on its rims and the sedan eased around town at 35 mph on ancient patched rubber and there was not enough extra gas that summer to even go to the beach.

But we fought on: we flattened tons of tin cans for tanks and salvaged kitchen fat for munitions and bundled high stacks of newspapers and magazines for who knows what. We bought a twenty-five cent savings stamp a week, and when the book was full it became a War Bond. On walks and walls we chalked our beliefs–*Hitler is a Heel*–and assertions of evolution–*Tojo is a Monkey's Uncle*. We said prayers, pledged allegiance, saluted the flag; and a thousand times our razored hate cheered John Wayne's single-handed assault against the Japs on Friday nights.

One bright morning when even the haze of war could not hide the sun, I came from behind the humped, tire-less coupe in the driveway and suddenly noticed the marsh land had become a profuse garden. The corn was a screen, thick as any bamboo grove, and below the tomatoes glowed red: tiny suns of Nippon. Bayonets of onion greens stabbed upward; potatoes, peppers, lettuce, carrots camouflaged the ground. Even the tarpaper shack seemed to stand a little straighter in the chaos of flowers, and its shutters and front door were painted bright yellow.

Sneaking through the foliage was the Jap: he was building tripods, small tent skeletons, for the beans.

Behind me Uncle Boswick came out, stretched, and surveyed the changed Technicolor landscape. He sported a new panama hat and two-tone perforated shoes, and I guessed that he was on his way to the USO club, although it was pretty early.

"Poppies," he said. "And not the kind the Legion sells."

I admired Uncle Boswick–I would never have thought of opium–and so I said yes, when he asked me to reconnoiter the area and to get some fresh vegetables, to be sent to his friends in Washington, D.C., for analysis. In spite of my father's order that the Jap be left alone, I wanted to get in the fight. Our fight. The rest of the day was spent with the Gang mapping out a plan of action. It was only after the details were settled that Slats mentioned it didn't get dark until nine, his bedtime. Our hoots and jeers at Slats were suddenly silenced when we realized that there wasn't one of us could stay out that late.

Therefore, at nine, as the sun fell beyond the muted, blacked out neon of Portland, I crawled from my bedroom window and slipped into the high grass. In the near-darkness I groped along the trench-work, and at the farthest OP I began to inch toward that garden on my stomach, a hunting knife clenched between my teeth. Near my face the chiirrruup of the crickets was deafening, and at every shift of my body the gas-mask bag slipped noisily; I paused to look back, and through the summer mist I saw the dull yellow cracks around black-out curtains in our frontroom, far away.

Crickets chirped nearby, an echo of bullfrogs farther out in the marsh, and along Johnson Creek the Galloping Goose cried into the night. A veil of wind blew a pungent, acrid green and then I saw the oiled, metallic sides of vegetables: cucumbers lay like small surface mines, aimed in every direction.

I waited, staring into the blackness at the tarpaper shack. Then the knife blade slipped across prickly stalks and three large specimens were in the bag. I crouched among the corrugated sides of squash, knife slashing, and moved quickly into the bayonets of green onions. Beyond were tomato plants, the hard black balls swimming in metallic greenness. Among the wide, sharp leaves of corn I was shielded, and it was not until the fourth ear had been split from its stalk that I felt a pang of fear. In the terror of silence leaf rasped on leaf. The knife was in my hand when I stood to stare into the silent, black night.

Not three plants away the Jap waited, arms folded, hat tipped to conceal his inscrutable face.

Even as I jumped I knew it must be a *scarecrow*—but I threw the knife overhand and flung away the gas-mask bag and ran across the misty, deep grass, the uneven ground falling away under my racing feet. Only when I was again in bed, rubbing my legs to stop their trembling, did I realize that the Jap had my knife—that he was now armed.

I slept with this fear and in a dream I heard voices at the back steps: "*Well they are lovely*" and "*Let me pay*" and "*I may keep the bag?*"

I heard the screen door open and my mother say "*Thankew*"— it was a trick no doubt—but then the door slammed shut and a figure passed outside my window. It shuffled under that same loose, flowing shirt and broad hat I had seen last night but again *I could not see any feature of the face.*

36

"Well, you're awake," my mother said. She was running water into a dishpan at the sink, and on the table, the gas-mask bag spilled out vegetables like a horn of plenty. "The Jap man gave us these," she said. "He wouldn't take any money, but I asked him to bring us some every week and I said I'd pay him a quarter— does that sound fair? He said he wants to buy some chickens."

Once a week until November the Jap came with a bag of produce, to accept my mother's money (as if there was no war on!), and to pass so close beneath the window that he must have felt the glow of my hatred.

He never did return my knife, either.

In what seemed the middle of summer, school began again. No matter that Paris and Guam and Palau had been liberated, or that bombs were falling on Manila, Luzon, and Okinawa, we marched into dull classrooms, carrying new notebooks already marked A.A.F.: we were all destined to become pilots, wearing white scarfs, chamois helmets, and leather jackets with the Flying Tiger patch on the back, like Errol Flynn. School for us was the twice-weekly War Communiqué film, where in the fluttering light we saw Patton tanks smash hedgerows, and bombs tumble like eggs toward the ultimate explosion. We squirmed with excitement as infantry charged across beaches strewn with dead and debris, as a flame-thrower sucked burning Japanese from caves, ending their ruthless mysticism. When the narrator's voice and the marching music ground to a halt and the projector stopped and the olive drab blinds were raised the boys would turn to look at one another and even Ellie Chombrake, the skinniest kid in the class, wore a sense of purpose on his face. The war was a common bond, holding us together; we all knew our role in this struggle for freedom.

Besides Christmas, only two things happened that school year.

One night in December, shortly before vacation, I was doing homework when I heard shouting in the field: it was The MacGregor.

From my front porch I heard him shouting crazily at the Jap and there was a distant crash of glass. I ran across the field, leaping trenches, until I saw the blurred outline of The MacGregor lobbing rock after rock at the tarpaper shanty; through the dark mist came the report of splintering boards. He was screaming and falling forward with every rock he threw, and I waited a minute before placing a hand on his shoulder. The face that turned was distorted into a crazy mask and I stepped back, but not quickly enough–his throwing fist, clutching a rock, came from the night to smash into my face.

It was father who helped us both home. and when he returned from The MacGregor's house, to hold an icepack against my bleeding cheek, he told us that Mr. MacGregor had been killed in what the newspapers celebrated as the Battle of the Bulge–where General McAuliffe said "nuts" to the Nazis. The telegram from the War Department assured Mrs. MacGregor that her husband had died a Hero.

My cheek no longer hurt: I felt good, and I wanted to shake The MacGregor's hand. But it was too late that night, my father said, and for the rest of the week The MacGregor's desk at school was empty, and by Saturday the mother and son had moved to Seattle, leaving a dark, lifeless house.

The next week, as if to replace our loss, Piggy's uncle sent home a large, olive drab box from the Pacific. Piggy was certain that it was a Christmas present for him but Gussie, his aunt, who was staying for the duration, said the box contained souvenirs, and that she had been instructed not to open it until Jed came home.

And within five minutes she had a crowbar against the lid, splintering wood; inside lay three long, dark rifles, a pistol wrapped in tan, oil-slick paper, and two Jap officer swords. Everything was coated with a thick rancid grease, but the guns were beautiful and the swords were works of art: they had scabbards crafted with inlaid wood and pearl, into which the delicate blade whispered. Gussie, who no doubt expected silks, hammered the lid back and from then on the basement was kept locked.

But for us, knowing those weapons were there, the war seemed much closer.

School was a huge wheel, grinding toward Spring. Its monotonous progress was interrupted only by the excitement of paper drives and tin can collections, practice blackouts and marches to the basement, which was now called the Air Raid Shelter. Here we huddled until the All Clear bell, discussing how we would fight the war when called, even though we could not see how it would last another eight years: the newspaper maps showed wide arrows, and by April the Americans and Russians were shaking hands in a defeated Berlin, while most of Europe was occupied by our boys. Although the Japanese were using *kamikazes* and Baka Bombs, Iwo Jima and Okinawa had been captured and it was only a matter of time before we would invade Japan itself.

Our winter had been mild and the spring rains turned the ground an energetic green. The trenches were hip-high in water, but from my bedroom window I watched the Jap at work seeding and hoeing. I wondered what he thought–surely he knew now that his country was defeated. A hundred short Japanese admirals were no match for one tall John Wayne marine. Why had he come here? What did he want? What was he working so hard for? No matter if he should again transform that wasteland into a blooming paradise, the whole neighborhood blotted him out with hate. Yet he foolishly worked on: feet bare, pants rolled to the knee, he dashed along the furrows in a lurching, forward-slanting crouch under the wide straw hat. When he was not working the land he was building the chicken coop, a temporary, tottering structure that made the tar-paper shack seem a palace. Apparently he had sold enough vegetables the previous summer, because one morning the fenced area was filled with small puffs of yellow, like frantic flowers. His dream was coming true, and I wanted to cross that field to make sure he understood that this could only happen in America–this was free enterprise, democracy.

The Jap had his chicks, V-E Day was celebrated, my dad was talking about the new car he would buy when this war was over, the neighborhood grew green, and school would soon end. It was into this spirit of optimism that Piggy's uncle returned.

If I had not seen him in uniform for a fleeting minute, as he walked from the car to the house that first day, I would not have believed that he had been in battle: all day, every day, he sat on the front porch in a rocking chair, wearing faded bib overalls and a brown shirt, and bearing no visible wound. He was a strange man with small, dull eyes and skin which became red without tanning; when he spoke his voice faded through short sentences, and he refused to talk about the War, even to Uncle Boswick.

"All he wants," said Uncle Boswick, "is to get back to that Alabama dirt farm, and sit."

"That's okay," my father said. "A man ought to own a bit of land."

"Gussie, now she's cut from a different bolt," Uncle Boswick said, winking. "I know her pretty well. She likes it here–plenty of ocean and forests and no niggers. Bet you five dollars she don't leave with him."

"Oh, now," my mother said, but her protest was weak for she had the gossip about Gussie straight from Piggy's mother: how Gussie had worked at Oregon Shipyard for two weeks after Jed had been shipped overseas. She had been back only for launchings, when the company gave out free beer and food, and we were told that any Saturday night she could be found along Harbor Drive, where ships on the Willamette tied up. Gussie, my mother said, was "wild" and "needed a baby to keep her home." Now that Jed was back she was sure that Gussie would "straighten out." Uncle Boswick, who seemed to know an awful lot about Gussie, said he wasn't so sure,

But rain or shine Jed remained in his rocking chair on the front porch, surveying the neighborhood with dull eyes. His uniform remained in the closet, and Piggy reported that Jed had gone into the basement only once to check the heavy box of souvenirs.

So we were surprised to see Gussie with the big samurai sword.

That late June sun was already an explosion of fire, burning life from the grass, but Piggy, Slats, Mike, and I worked in the trenches anyway; we felt needed, for after V-E Day the war focused on the Pacific, our ocean. We repaired trench walls where the rains had worn them away, and filled sandbags, piled our rocks, and sometimes lobbed an occasional missile at the Jap's chicken coop—but half-heartedly, for now that we knew Tojo was finished our Jap seemed more like a docile intruder: unwanted, but harmless. Uncle Boswick had even taken to crossing the field two or three times a week, to "interrogate" the Jap about when the hens would start laying. For eggs were still rationed.

I trained Uncle Boswick's binoculars on the Jap's shack, then slowly swept them across the chicken coop. the vast garden—for I wanted to see my enemy's face, to see if in these last days of the war that face could maintain its humorless intensity—when at my elbow Slats said: "What's that noise?"

All I heard was Gussie's radio. Whenever she was sunbathing her radio blared hot hillbilly music into the quiet neighborhood. But today she was not sunbathing. When I swung the binoculars past our house to Piggy's backyard, I saw Gussie in the far corner wearing tiny shorts and halter.

The noise that Slats heard was the blackberry vines being chopped, and what Gussie was using was the big Jap sword.

She was working, and I recalled what my mother had said about Gussie "straightening out" with Jed home. It was the first time I had ever seen her do work of any kind. Like Uncle Boswick, she did not need to work.

We charged from the trench, knowing that long wooden box of war souvenirs was lying open in an unlocked basement. But Piggy said: "If we wait for Jed, he'll show them to us."

Under the hot sun we waited while on that porch Jed rocked, his eyes focused on something above the rooftops, and in the far corner of the yard the sword flashed like a mirror. We waited, wondering how many American boys' heads that long blade spilled on Bataan, Corrigedor, Wake Island, and for the blade each time that Gussie hit a rock. Through the binoculars I watched Jed's face, dull and impassive, and finally I saw the lips tighten slowly, pulling his eyes narrow. Suddenly the field of vision was filled with his striped bib-overalls. I lowered the glasses to see Jed stand up; he spit once over the porch rail, scratched his seat, and started down the steps as we charged from the trench.

Jed walked slowly past the basement door, down the driveway, and was blotted from sight by our house. We were halfway to the road when Jed re-appeared, to take the sword from Gussie.

Later I was unsure exactly what I saw—we were still a good distance away, and it happened very fast. She had the sword raised overhead in both hands, to assault the tenacious blackberry vines, when Jed stepped from behind and grabbed the blade. The surprise of his movement sent her spinning off balance, and she fell among the daggers of the vines. We heard her cry once—a single, abrupt noise and saw the blade flash, an arc of sunlight across our eyes, forever impressed. An irregular, stunned line of boys watched in horror as Jed came from behind the trees and the obstructing house; he lurched toward that cool dark basement.

We retreated to the trench. where I exchanged one nervous glance with Piggy: Gussie lay in the vines, pumping her blood out, and beyond that dark recessed doorway Jed had the guns. We gripped the lip of the turf, not even pretending to arm ourselves with throwing stones, until we heard the thin siren droning from Lents, an insect in the hot afternoon; and at the same instant a muffled explosion churned up from that basement, growing like a cloud to envelop the neighborhood.

A few minutes after Uncle Boswick jumped the fence which separated Piggy's yard from mine; the police car raced to the curb. As the officers moved up the driveway, guns thrust into the yard's calm, we raced to the road and saw Uncle Boswick point to that far corner. Blood smudged his shirt, and his eyes slanted against tears—at the time, it was my impression that he had cut himself coming over the fence.

And before the policemen came back from viewing Gussie's slim, decapitated body, and before Uncle Boswick chased us into the street, we gathered at the small, dirt spattered basement window: Jed was sitting in the corner, propped against the dirt wall by the Jap rifle. The big toe of his right foot was hooked into the trigger guard; the barrel pointed into the darkness where half his head was missing. Behind him a fan-shaped stain drew flies.

The deaths were not mentioned that evening at supper, a meal eaten in silence; but later, on the front steps, Uncle Boswick announced, as if I did not already know:

"He did it with the *sam-yer-eye* sword. Can you believe that? Ahhhh, she was a beautiful girl." He went on, in a voice charged with amazed indignation, to tell how he had seen the blade flash once across the sun from the chaise lounge in our back yard; he thought it was a dream. From that moment his world was one of missing pieces, of edges that never did quite meet, and when I asked him again what really had happened all he could say was: "He did it with the *sam-yer-eye*."

But that was not what I wanted to know.

Nor did the Jap make any sense to him. A few days after the deaths Uncle Boswick crossed that wasteland to "interrogate" the Jap, and when he returned his voice was charged with amazed fury. "The hens are finally laying, but he ain't eating the eggs. The Jap ain't eating the eggs and he won't sell them. I'm telling you the whole world's gone nuts."

After Uncle Boswick left for the USO club, I got out his binoculars and my plane spotter's manual—for four years I had been searching the skies for a Zero or Mitsubitsi bomber. From the blue skies I lowered the glasses to focus on the Jap's shack, and for the first time I noticed that the profusion of flowers had shrunk back into the mud. The shack leaned to its own shadow; a yellowed newspaper fluttered from the window broken long ago by The MacGregor's stone. I shifted to the garden out back, and saw corn burned by the sun fold into stiff stalks, diminishing like candle wax.

The glasses focused on the slanting assemblage of wood and wire, and although the nests were concealed I could see the slumps of dirty white which flashed from corners: the hens had begun to lay their eggs in any depression. I slowly swung the glasses across the Jap's property–scanning every inch of peeling paint, broken glass, and browned foliage–but I saw no sign of the Jap. The chickens milled about the dusty arena, without food or water, eyeing each other suspiciously.

The eggs began to pile up, dropped from the starving, wiry hens, and I knew this was another fiendish, exquisite eastern torture. I pictured the Jap hiding in a corner of the shack, drunk on sake, giggling his sharp-toothed, rat-faced fanaticism.

The eggs piled up, delicate and white, and every day Uncle Boswick crossed that wasteland to beg, plead, argue the Jap into selling him some eggs. I would watch Uncle Boswick cross the field and stand by the bottom step of the porch; I could see his mouth moving, hands flying–but I never saw the Jap. Only a shadow across the broken window, a faint movement which might have been the curtain blowing. On any day during the past year he would have been running on short admiral legs across the tilled soil, a water bucket in each hand, or he would have been leaning on his shovel, or kneeling over seeds, as if in prayer. Now he did not come out of the tar-paper shack, not even to feed the chickens.

It was not until two weeks later, when the heat of summer shifted into August, that Uncle Boswick was able to learn why the Jap refused to part with his eggs.

Uncle Boswick was trying to talk my mother into going across that field to plead with the Jap. "You've got to go–the egg route is all sewn up, I've got customers. We've got to make some money soon, before this war is over. Gawd knows every businessman has lined his nest: the junk-yards selling gas tamps and tires from wrecks at black-market prices, the gas stations, the meat markets–they're getting rich!"

We had never had any money, and he was trying to appeal to her only fear: poverty. But apparently she feared the Jap even

44

more, for she would not go—not even when he told her what he had learned.

"Do you know why he won't do anything with them?" Uncle Boswick asked. "He bought the chickens so he could have some eggs—and now he tells me he can't eat the eggs of hens he knows personally. That he has fed with his own hands. *Hens he knows personally!*"

For Uncle Boswick this was the ultimate puzzle, and he abandoned his attempt to collaborate with the enemy. Other afternoons would be spent in the chaise lounge, warming his war wounds against the sun, clipping money-making advertisements from magazines.

But I continued to watch the drama of torture with a strange fascination: every morning I went to the foxhole and focused binoculars on the chicken coop, where lean hens milled, eyeing each other suspiciously. Their high wiry bodies bobbed and crowded as they rotated in an endless circle under the blazing sun. I saw those near the fence stretch through the wire, their hysterical beaks reaching for any green leaf.

One day toward noon, just as I was about to return home for lunch, I saw a hen squat in the dust and when it rose, the quizzical eye aimed at the sun, its dusty, hoarse clucking was suddenly strangled. The hen's head darted like a wedge; the sharp beak smashed the shell, and the hen began to devour her own egg.

From the side another hen kicked high into the air, wings flapping, mad with the smell of food. A cloud of feathers exploded over the oily yolk as the two fought—others jumped in, and mass hysteria spread like the rising dust cloud. I watched with excited horror, for I had been waiting for something like this—the dust, torn feathers, the savage choked cries. From behind the wire a gas cloud rose, and the smell of rotten eggs drifted on the wind, an ominous yellow cloud which would stain every house, touch every life.

Fifteen minutes later, when the air was fairly clear, I could see that every egg had been pecked open.

Again the tide rotated wing to wing, hungry for food, space, the freedom of flight. They pressed together tightly, accelerating in a small circle within the confines of the wire until motion became a brown blur. Their movement held no hope for escape, but the smell of food had driven them mad and this was a kind of direct action—in desperation their yellow feet raced across the baked earth, the head at the end of the arched neck in pursuit of something. I waited, watching with that same sense of excited horror I had known the day Jed walked off the porch and the morning the Jap had first appeared on our horizon.

Then, near the wire, one stumbled with exhaustion. Her wings fanned the dust, but before she could rise, the beak of her neighbor slashed out. She struggled, her chalky cluuuk filled with urgency and alarm, but from the circle's momentum a dozen hens peeled off and were on her, necks extended, beaks chopping at her eyes.

When two of the attackers drew back, their dusty feathers were speckled with blood. Through binoculars I could see the stained hens lift their wings, crane their necks at a difficult angle to drink off the beads of blood. Behind them the circle began to disintegrate, and the smell of blood carried to my foxhole as hens surrounded to attack the attackers.

Originally there were perhaps thirty chickens, and the next day when I returned there were half that number. On the third day there were ten, and then five walked among the debris of feathers and bones. These five had grown heavy, nourished by the fallen, and they waddled grotesque and wary. One stayed in each corner of the coop, and one paced a small circle in the center.

Later there were only two left, and these had been changed until they looked more like buzzards—their necks were plucked bare, and what lower feathers remained had turned black from the blood and dust. Seen through the binoculars the birds looked arrogant, fierce, and utterly mad. Their feet were claws and their heads like hatchets, topped by the blood-filled comb. Each preened and arched in her space, proud that she had survived. I wondered whether inside the shack the Jap was giggling or filled with revulsion—after all, these were hens he had known personally.

And suddenly the War was over.

On our small street people spilled from houses, cheering and shouting, touching one another. My mother, after saying a prayer to God, even smoked a cigarette in her excitement, and there was cold beer on the table. The cloud of War had lifted. Relief and happiness passed through our house like a seismic wave. From the radio came the official details: *At 12:01 The Great Artiste dropped the second bomb…a pillar of fire, 10,000 feet high, shot skyward with enormous speed, moving to become a mushroom shaped cloud which eventually attained a height of 60.000 feet… officials estimate that the blast caused extensive damage…*

The War had ended. In that room I sensed a curious mixture of gladness and despair, as if we were suddenly released from what had held us together. I could not recall a time before Pearl Harbor. I could only remember a world at war, and all my energy for four years had been consumed by the war effort—I'd spent hundreds of hours digging the home defenses, scanning the sky for enemy aircraft, watching war communiqué films at school. I had collected tons of waste paper, tin cans, old cooking fat. I had grown Victory gardens, stayed up nights watching for tire thieves, helped my mother to keep the OPA Consumer's Pledge.

"Jesus." Uncle Boswick heard the news and his hand reached for another cold beer.

My father had his bank book out, and was searching the columns with a scowl. The War had killed the Depression, moving him into the only prosperity he'd ever known. He'd wet the pencil tip against his tongue and began to figure on an old envelope, moving into peace half-heartedly.

I walked to the street's edge and looked both ways, as if I might see that cresting mushroom cloud, or be touched by its gigantic shadow. For the war had touched us all: I thought of The MacGregor, Gussie, and Jed—in the dark enigma of that basement, that stained wall, I later realized we had viewed every casualty.

And in the field where we had labored hard and well, grass already grew in our trenches.

Perhaps because the Jap was no longer my enemy, but more likely because I was curious of the face I had never seen, I walked slowly through the yielding high grass toward the leaning tarpaper shack. Against the broken window the old newspaper floated, the type erased by sun and wind. Closer, I saw that the shutters threatened to fall from rusty hinges, and that their bright yellow paint had now curdled into rivulets. My knock was timid, and unanswered, but the door was ajar and I could see through the single room to the backyard.

The house was empty. Any furniture the Jap might have had was gone, and so as he. There was not even the smell of soy sauce, nor the odor of yellow; not even a grain of rice captured in the floor's parallel cracks remained as evidence. I stood in the tiny room, where dust motes drifted like dandelion fuzz across the sun's scorching shafts, and I wondered where he had gone. I wanted him to see my triumph—we had won, Japan was conquered. Also, I wanted to see his face—just once, up close, to see if he wasn't an exact copy of the grinning monkey the magazines had shown us. Where was he? Had he committed hari-kari in the garden?

The only evidence that the empty room had been lived in recently were the newspapers covering one wall. Bold headlines jumped from the yellow paper; the print faded into blurred words, columns of statistics, tracing the war's progress—down to the two day old newspaper taped at a crazy angle in the corner, its ink still firm.

Under the low ceiling the August heat collected; thick blue flies hummed furiously in the hot air, and as I walked out the back door it occurred to me that the Jap's departure would really baffle Uncle Boswick.

The garden was leveled; except for the small, open dirt mound, a row of scabs where the corn had been, all traces of the Jap's industry were sucked into the baked earth. A few loose feathers drifted across the space where last year cucumbers had lain in profusion, like surface mines, and the night air had been

48

green with the metallic darkness of hard, fist-sized tomatoes. The feathers drifted from the rotting pile within the chicken coop, mute testimony to the destruction. The ground within the wire was perforated with the puck marks of claws, littered with bleached, dry bones. From inside the shed came a brittle noise, and I wondered if there could be a survivor—I had imagined those last two hens fighting by moonlight until each had driven a slashing, crescent beak into the other. The noise—a chewing, tearing sound—continued, and I searched the baked earth for a handful of grass, to throw over the wire fence.

As the grass drifted down, each blade flashing like a knife, the burlap cover at the small doorway moved. Then the single remaining chicken emerged. She dashed across the enclosure on thick legs to where the blades were still falling; cautiously, she sniffed at my offering but did not touch it—she had acquired a taste for blood.

The angular, massive head turned and behind deep folds her fierce eyes were fixed on me; with a crouching run she accelerated, to crash heavily into the wire. Her thick, short neck absorbed the impact, and she moved back, grunting, to try again. Her rush had carried the terrific odor of fowl, blood, dung, dust; and with this stink in my nose I now saw that she had lost all of her feathers and the skin was a silky black, broken only by the white scars. Grown short and fat, the crescent beak hooked like a primitive tooth, she had metamorphosed into a kind of rat.

Of the flock, this was the Victor.

Conversation with My Father

Our elbows steady the table's curb;
Our palms hold our thoughts. We glare
Over a glass of beer, over generations,
And my inquiry is a protest:
—You mean, the 'twenties and 'thirties?
The joys of the Jazz Age: where men
In undershirts dealt cards below a ten-
Watt bulb, drank whisky neat, and played
The radio, Naive as Lum and Abner.
Where Keaton and Chaplin walked:
Wide rutted roads, without sidewalks,
Faced funny clapboard houses, and parked
Six cars in twice as many blocks.
Of uncomplicated wars; unregimented moods,
To the lawless extreme of Dillinger.
When anything was possible, like the Model T
Running primly upright to ford a new epoch.
Those good times, mirrored now in the sweet
Serenity of the late late show:
You mean it wasn't so?
—No, he sighs. Unable to explain he stares
At where our glasses stained the table,
The interlocking rings like other worlds.
—No, he says, it weren't.

Tillamook Burn

Since before my memory these stumps
have stood commemorating a bronze plaque:
grotesque inland driftwood.
The hills roll back, grass returns;
trunks track history in rings,
mark the burn that pulled trestles
from logging trains; and pegged in place
these ashes can withstand the worst Oregon rains.

I think my father fought that fire.
I know he skinned cat for the WPA
out here, clubbed jack-salmon in Wolf Creek,
came home weekends smelling of woods.
I see him in our bare living room,
in high-laced boots, hat rimmed with union pins
He brings another case of soup; a kiss
for mother. In the chair he sits
in pipe smoke reading a pulp western,
or mows the lawn.
                              And then he's gone.

Memory is mixed truth and dreams.
But times I've returned from Seaside,
hung-over, mouth black as a stump,
mind gritty from sleeping on the beach—
after these wild drunks I've seen him rise
in flame on a ridge: he's fought that fire
night and day; alone, mustache singed,
he mocks the inferno. He works for no pay,
nor does he care about lost board feet,
headlines, the WPA. or the world.
A super-figure in a labor mural consumed
by work in a world burnt brown—
what he had he shared, gave away, and got

mistakes which flared like pine-knots,
and a burnt-out stump for a heart—
a brief hot flame;
for this there is no bronze plaque, only ashes,
broken places.

Ambush

Fed on chemicals this park grass springs
too green; the high firs have shrunk.
The past returns examples of deceit—
tricks of memory, a cropped photo.
a puzzle scattered and incomplete.

Yet under these diminished trees
the last notes of the big band sound
carry on the breeze from the radio
in a car that seems too square;
from every mother's kitchen steak
fills the air; and in the paperbags
that slap my bike's rear wheel I stare
at twenty year old headlines.

The swings still struggle in their chains.
Sprinkler hoses lie coiled to strike.
But this park and I have changed; on bars
other monkeys play, risk falls, broken bones
and future limps, ignorant how the body
becomes an old house, pipes rattling in walls.
Against the slide's bright metal a decade fades:
the evening hangs eternal in summer mist,
before sunset a paper finds each porch
and after dinner my father and I sit
on steps in his pipe smoke scheming
tomorrow's separate strategies.
His vision is grand. from magazine ads
he dreams himself independent, free,

owner of his own work-bench, a garage
where his week shortens to six long days.
He no doubt includes me in his plan.
Drake & Son, but I am thinking of the Sudan,
the Foreign Legion, the shape of Mexico;
my hero is Richard Halliburton, my wall map
pinned with places I must go when I skip
this neighborhood. I want to test my fear
of death: five times I've read *Beau Geste*,
and see myself dying well, far from here,
fighting against the infidel. Or best,
to return scarred by ticker-tape parades.

These dreams fade with pipe-smoke into dusk;
the myths remain in books I read, try to write.
Hard work got my father that garage,
a dream elusive but American; when he'd pumped
his life out like gas we borrowed the money
to bury him. For me, desert sands still stretch
vast and trackless.
                          Yet what changes could
save us from our ends? The present is past
too soon, old jokes; time, confetti, is tossed
on parades of days for whatever we can celebrate:
a broken business, a ruined heart;
or an inch of library shelf, a file card
as epitaph: *Collected Works,* 1 Vol.,
as empty as this park.

The Summer of Sad Cars

That summer seemed like a mad drive toward some distant place, a city bathed in neon, but later he realized the shimmering vision was a mirage, that he had not got anywhere, and that all that driving had left a trail of cars scattered along roads like the leaves of fall.

His father's Lincoln Zephyr went first, wounded within. Then his Buick, dying in the heat from old age. The 1935 Ford sedan, the Oldsmobile with its primitive Hydra-Matic, a Studebaker coupe, a 1938 Ford, a 1936 Chevrolet—they stretched in a row like the final result of a long assembly line, windshields winking as they waited for the scrapper.

Why had he wasted them? They wanted to know. Why had they failed him? He wanted to know.

The Lincoln was a huge boat of a car, black paint faded and chipped, but his father thought it had class—meaning the twin spotlights, the underseat heaters, the push-button doors. It's the kind of car an executive would drive, his father might have said, but to Chris' hot rage the car had no power. The original V-12 engine gulped gas to produce its own smokescreen, and so his father replaced it with a V-8. Overweight and underpowered, it would barely get out of its own way. Like everything else, Chris thought, it limped along.

He drove it everywhere, sitting behind the wheel like an owner. School had ended in May, when his father came home sick, and Chris went to work in the service station. It was to be a couple of days, then a week, but time stretched into the beautiful weather of June and when school had officially ended he was still pumping gas, doing oil changes and lube jobs, the grime etched into the lines of his hands. By then he had already wasted three cars.

One night, he picked up his father's medicine at the Rexall, and when he came out Buzz was beside the fender with two girls. He heard the laughter, saw the cigarette's glow, and then Buzz whispered that they were hot to trot, and did he want to drive to

58

The Point? Chris looked at the medicine in his hand and then at the two girls–thin shadows beside the car–and, heart racing said, "Why not?" They got in, a girl beside each boy, and as he started the car, pulling away from Lents, she said: "Whatcher name? I'm Sally."

"I'm Chris," he said. The name sounded strange–was that who he was? In the dark countryside they had come to he wondered where he was going, what he was going to be. Sally's leg was against his, her perfume choked the air. Her presence, the way she lit her cigarette excited him and he wanted to think about anything except the service station.

"Yer in school?" she asked, exhaling thin streams from her nose.

"I'm out," he said, as if he had already graduated; as if this long black Lincoln gliding through the night on fat whitewall tires were his.

"Yar", she said. "Me too–I'm car-hopping at Merhars."

The road turned, inclined toward the blinking lights of the radio station high on Mt. Scott, and at its base was The Point. Chris stepped the gas to the floor, heard the carburetor's gasp. They sped upward, the city unfolding beneath them in a carpet of lights; the carb sucked, gasped, they climbed into thinner air and headlights clipped off the white headstones of the cemetery.

"Yer cute, y'know it?" Sally said, moving closer, his arm was draped around her back and waist, and with one hand he guided the Lincoln's great white wheel, steering upward, In the mirror he saw Buzz kiss his girl, and Chris wasn't sure he would know how to kiss–he had never had to–but he would try, for the pressure of warm lips was what he wanted.

As the road inclined sharply the car grew weary, slowed. Chris reached with his free hand to shift to second, felt the back end bounce, the fat tires accept the new gear. Under the wide expanse of hood, the engine whined, straining.

"Oh don'tcha just love it up here?" Sally said, leaning back, her breasts catching the highlights from the dash. She was agreeable to anything, he thought, and as the car began to buck, slow, he shifted into low and cursed.

59

"This crate gonna make it?" Buzz wondered. The car began the final mile of hill and halfway up, engine screaming, the speedometer needle dropping to the small numbers. Half a mile separated them from the top when the Lincoln bucked to a stop.

"Wait," Chris said, "I'll try again."

He coasted down in reverse, half-turned with his leg firmly against Sally, her eager warmth entering him. He coasted back to the final turn, gunned the engine, popped the clutch, and the heavy car lunged into the night. He left it in low, his foot to the floor all the way, lights clipping the grave markers with rapid flashes. Then the car stuttered, and a thin whisper of steam traced from under the broad hood and again it bucked, shuddered, clicked metallic through the drive train, the rear wheels, and all power dissolved.

"Oh shit," Sally said.

"Let's walk it," Buzz said.

"No," Chris said, for it was a matter of pride, this being his very first date with a girl. "I'll try it in reverse."

Again he backed down the hill, and at the first curve turned the car around.

Engine now cool, he gunned it, popped clutch and hanging from the door he guided the big car through the night in reverse. The giant wheel rocked in his hands, steering the dancing swaths of red, the tail lights an echo of the radio tower lights high over The Point. It was difficult, speeding in reverse into darkness; he wished that his father had let him clip a red and chrome squirrel-knob on the wide white wheel.

The gas pedal mushed underfoot, the carb gasped, balked; all power turned to jello within the chrome-hard cylinder walls–the rear wheels turned slower, began to hop against the road in excited convulsions as the grade steepened. In desperation Chris popped the clutch in and out, the engine racing full throttle for a second then fading into the driving wheels. Suddenly he felt the clutch pedal fall to the floor, dead–something within had broken, like a bone slipped from its socket–and slowly the car began to coast downhill, into the city.

Looking across the Buick's hood Chris watched the traffic on Sandy Boulevard—the bright chrome and paint, cars which moved as smoothly as the owners' lives. Almost every one he could identify by make, model, year. Occasionally he would see a hybrid, a sleek custom job easing along, lowered hip-high, skirts, dual exhausts, everything he dreamed of.

His father came from the clinic, went down the steps carefully, and walked with exaggerated slowness across the parking lot. His hat brim was tipped across his forehead, and his leather jacket was scuffed into light and dark patterns. When he got to the car it seemed that he took forever getting the door open and with infinite patience he stepped on the running board, sat down slowly, then pulled in his feet. Finally he shut the door.

"Uuhhh," he said, "that lug thinks I'm a pincushion."

Chris had the engine running, and the big Buick moved across the lot and into the street. The differential had the bearing howl common to GM cars, but Chris had poked a hole in the muffler and the rumble of exhaust covered all other noises. He had bought it for ten dollars, replaced the timing chain, and had intended to sell it; now however, he had nothing else to drive. In moments of wild fantasy he thought about putting four Strombergs on it, milling the head, and splitting the exhaust manifold. It would make a good tow car, if he ever decided to race the roadster.

"Let's get a cone," his father said.

"Sure," he said, stopping at Miller's 33 Flavors; these drives were like going on a picnic, he thought. A hot breeze bounced off the asphalt but inside it was cool; the girl behind the counter wore a fuchsia-colored uniform and he could see through it to the lines of her underwear. He wished that his hands were not so dirty. He ordered a double dip chocolate cone for his father and a rocky road for himself, and they sat in the car eating them. This stop had become a ritual in their weekly drive to the clinic, and Chris wondered whether his father did it as a reward for Chris or because he enjoyed breaking the doctor's strict diet.

"Well, that sawbones says I can go back to work." He had a thin line of ice cream along the line of his mustache.

61

"Great," Chris said, thinking about his roadster spread in a million pieces in the basement of the garage. If he had, say, a hundred dollars and two weeks uninterrupted time, he believed he could have that car back on the road.

The following Monday his father rode with him in the Buick, their lunch pails together on the seat between them. Chris trembled with excitement as he drove down the clean rain-swept streets. Traffic was light and he drove smoothly as Woodstock curved into the plush Reed campus and around the golf course; as they followed the river south, his excitement mounted, and he wondered at his heart pounding.

At the garage, he put out the displays, unlocked the pumps, opened the wide doors while his father looked around the office. By nine, before the day became hot, he was ready to duck downstairs to work on his car. He was studying the situation when his father came to the top of the stairs and called him. "Chris, fellow wants his oil checked."

He came up the stairs, wiping his hands on a rag and walked past his father to the pump island. The car was a new Olds 88, and now that he had come all the way out here, Chris did not mind opening the hood to get a look at that engine. "Doc says I wasn't supposed to lift anything heavy," his father explained to the driver, leaning toward the window. "That means hoods too. I'm not supposed to put my hands over my head."

Jeezus christ, thought Chris, shutting it, nodding to the driver that the oil level was fine. If he can't lift a hood I'll be up here all the time. His father got the money and rang it up, walking around the car with a terrible slowness. Chris looked down the street, and admired a bright maroon Ford convertible that rumbled past; he hated the kid who drove it, top down, toward the swimming area of the lake.

Most of the morning, Chris was in the lube room or on the island. His father disappeared from time to time, emerging later from that grimy green cubicle they called a bathroom. "I keep having to pee," he said, trying to laugh. "But nothing happens." They ate lunch together in the office; Chris was finished while his father still nibbled on a sandwich, chewing with the same slowness that characterized his walk. Chris latched his lunch bucket, got a drink of water from the yellowed fountain outside and rested against the doorjamb.

"Say Chris," his father said, "Maxie will buy the front spring off that '37 Ford if we take it off–says he'll come by before five."

Chris looked at the clock and said, "Guess I better go now." He got a tray of tools, a floor jack and went down the hill to the field behind the garage. A dozen cars sat in the high grass, overgrown by blackberry vines; his father had hauled them here one at a time, and although the city council was trying to stop him, he was junking the cars for parts. Chris jacked up the front end of the coupe, blocked the axle, and crawled under. The grass was hot and dusty, but the shade below the front fender was cool. He wire-brushed the spring shackles, squirted them with Liquid Wrench, and waited; black and yellow bees big as his thumb droned through the berry vines, and the odor of sunbaked paint, engine oil, dusty grass saturated everything. Lying on his back he could see the blue sky beyond the bumper– what if he had his car together? he wondered. What if his father hadn't been–wasn't–sick? Last summer had been a dream; he had worked on his car in the warm sun, reading magazines and drinking lemonade in the hammock when it got too hot. He and Horace went downtown, went to the Aero Theater on Friday nights, had mock battles as a dreamy dusk fell around the neighborhood.

He squirted the shackles again, then pounded them to break the rust's grip; he got the nuts off one side but a shackle bolt on the other side stripped. He began to chisel it off when his father called. He got out from under dust and grass chaff irritating his skin, and ran down the hill. "He wants his oil checked." With exaggerated speed, Chris opened the hood, checked the oil, closed it, and ran back down the hill. He chiseled the nut off but couldn't get the shackle free of the spring; he jacked and blocked, trying to ease the spring's tension, but the shackles were frozen. He lay in the hot grass, sweating, dirt impressed into his cheek, and then with all his strength he swung the hammer; the shackle

63

didn't budge. He swung again and as the hammer head deflected his knuckles hit the frame horn, peeling back the skin.

His father called again, and Chris came to the top, sweaty and dusty. "Listen," he said, motioning with his thumb, "I can't keep running up and down the hill. It's all loose, you get it off." He went to the island and checked the oil in Bartegan's old Hudson; it was down the usual quart and he also sold her a pint of clutch fluid, knowing that it too would be down. When Bartegan left Chris walked into the road and looked at where the grass was flattened beneath the '37 Ford. Then he saw the door of the Buick was open and from it stretched a pair of legs; when he walked over to it he saw his father sleeping in the back seat, hat tipped over his face against the sun.

Chris bought a bottle of Coke and squatted near the door, enjoying the small breeze that drifted through the shade beneath the wooden canopy. Shit, he thought without anger, this wasn't the way he figured it would be.

His father didn't come back again, and for the rest of the summer Chris drove to work alone, ate lunch in the office alone, each evening he headed toward home, another day done.

A week later the Buick quit; he was halfway up the steep grade above Reed College when the car slowed, then began to coast backward, the engine racing. An axle? he wondered: transmission? clutch? He left it angled into the curb–a rat gray sedan with a crumpled fender and a hood he had never quite got on correctly–and it sat in that posh neighborhood for weeks until he finally got it hauled home.

He hitchhiked to the station the next day, arriving at noon. Between customers he carried a battery and a can of gas down the hill and picked out a car from the junkers; a 1935 Ford sedan, trunk model. It was solid, with fair upholstery, and complete; only after he got it running and started up the hill did he realize that the clutch slipped badly. He gave it a quick wash, hung on license plates from the Buick, and parked it across the street. He studied it, imagining a nice green paint job, whitewalls, skirts; it began to look better and better.

The next week, when he drove his father to the clinic, he said, "I think we can fix it up, don't you? We got those mufflers, we could put on duals. Lower it." Because he was getting sick of the garage, of days passing in the grime of the lube rack; because he wanted to be free on the streets with his friends, he tried to believe that this car could be made not only beautiful but perfect. "What do you think?"

"I think it needs a new clutch," his father said.

His father sat stiffly beside the door, looking straight ahead. He looked smaller, shrinking into his clothes, and his skin seemed yellowish. That was due to a lack of sunshine, Chris assumed. His father hardly went out of the house; he spent the day sleeping or sitting in a chair in the front room, reading westerns and mysteries. Chris' mother gave the shots, bathed him, gave alcohol rubs and watched his diet. The one thing she couldn't do was to make him stop smoking; he smoked Luckies constantly and when they were gone he rolled his own or took out a pipe.

"We'll stick in a new clutch." Chris said.

"There's a reason," his father said, breathing heavily. "Probably the rear main leaks." The words came with effort, but he kept his voice level as if he were a teacher. "Wouldn't do no good to put in a new disc and pressure plate. Have to put in a new lower end. This had babbitted rods—"

"Okay!" Chris said, stepping on the gas in anger; the clutch slipped and the engine over-revved wildly until he let up.

"That don't do it no good."

"Okay, forget it." Chris said. "Who cares."

"Gee, I wish you hadn't broken the Lincoln."

At the clinic Chris waited in the car, studying its dashboard and interior; he hated the clinic, with its overpowering medicinal smells and the rows of crippled and sick arranged along the walls. In the car he could watch traffic and dream, floating within a cloud that promised only good things.

Eventually his father came out the door, looked around, and used the handrail to help himself down the stairs. He walked more slowly than ever, and when he got to the door he said: "Why didn'tcha park closer?"

"Can't see the road." Chris said, hitting the starter button even before his father was seated. The starter growled and almost immediately the solenoid clicked against the firewall. Either the battery was dead or a terminal was loose; Chris got out, raised the hood side and tapped the connection with a wrench while his father stood, half in and half out, waiting. He tried the starter button again but nothing happened. "We got to push it. I guess." he said, trying to see which direction was at least level if not downhill; everything looked upward to him, as if they had parked over a water drain.

"Hells bells." He put the gear lever in neutral, then went to the back. "Well, let's try to go that way."

His father looked at the car and the direction in which Chris had gestured; he took a deep breath, as if reaching a decision. "Don't think I can," he said. "I can't."

Chris waited, palms against the hot metal, looking at his father; he sure as hell couldn't push it alone. But the choice was to try or sit there for hours or to call a tow truck. "Well, shoot," he said, "maybe you could at least steer it toward that driveway."

He could see through the rear window as his father got in, slid across the seat, and as Chris leaned against the trunk anger shot adrenalin through his system. Feet braced, he pushed with his shoulder and the car inched forward picking up speed when it surged down the driveway the V-8 staggered to life, missed, then caught. Chris ran ahead and as his father slid across the seat he got behind the wheel, foot on the pedal; he was breathing heavily and had to wait until his heart quit pounding.

"Gonna stop for a cone?" his father said. "Leave the car running while you go in. "

"No time," he said. He did have to be back to work, but there was time to stop. He had said that because he was angry about the car.

"Oh come on," his father said. "It won't take long. Please."

He stepped on the gas, listened to the engine wind up without moving them any faster, shifted quickly into second gear; oil

66

smoke pumped through the holes in the firewall, enveloping them in a bluish cloud. When they got to Miller's 33 flavors, he pulled up to the curb, angled the back tire against it, and ran inside with the engine running. As the girl dipped into the bins he recalled that his father had said please–Chris felt a kind of power, as if he were the head of the family.

But he didn't want power or responsibility–he wanted simple things, he wanted his car running and to be free to run around nights with Hop and Buzz and the others, and to not be so damn tired that all he could do was crawl into bed, falling into a dreamless sleep. There had to be more than days passing, like leaves falling from a calendar or a colorless column moving past his eyes, one day exactly like the others. He wanted to find those girls again, and to try to get to The Point.

Saturday night Murphy, Hop, Buzz, and Bill stopped in front of his house. He had just finished dinner when the horn honked and he went to the window, to see a bright yellow convertible at the curb. Buzz yelled,"C'mon out." He quickly slipped into Levis and a blue shirt and was heading out the door when his parents came into the front room, his mother supporting his father.

"I'll be back soon." he said.

He came down the steps and walked around the convertible. It was bright yellow, with brown leather upholstery. "Hey man. where'd you get this?"

"Traded the Merc in," Murphy said. "you like it?"

"You bet," Chris said, imagining himself cruising Foster Road in this. He would have even settled for Murphy's old Mercury, which had a leopard skin headliner that drove girls wild.

"Well, let's go, Buzz said.

"Where to?" Chris asked, hitching up his pants, opening the convert's door and sitting in the rich leather; the door sill just fitted under his arm.

"Who knows?" Murphy said, lighting a cigarette. "Let's see what's shaking." That suited Chris, and what happened was that they cruised the main streets, the top down, the wind sweeping their heads; Chris loved the way people looked at them, envied them—the garage was forgotten, he was moving into a whole new world. Girls waved, eager to be seen. They cruised until it got dark, then went to the 82nd Street Drive-In; Murphy played his spotlight across the empty screen, and when the film started they sat in the open, under the stars, watching the figures on the big screen, watching lovers in other cars, talking and horsing around, eating popcorn and drinking Cokes. Chris remembered that last year they had come here in Buzz's father's pickup, hiding in the back behind large cardboard boxes until they were inside the fence and then bursting out to sit on the hood and fenders. Chris felt older this summer and couldn't imagine acting that way.

After the films they joined the long line of cars and cruised slowly down 82nd, toward Merhar's. Chris felt terribly conspicuous and even important as they cruised through and pulled into an empty space; everyone was looking at them. Murphy left his lights on until a car-hop came across the parking lot, hips swaying "Hiya, doll," Murphy said, making his eyes thin; he talked around his cigarette, trying to look like Dean Martin. "Well, what'll it be, men?"

They all got coffee and fries, and Murphy ordered a hamburger. He had quit school two years before and had a good job in n warehouse; he could afford convertibles, cigarettes, and hamburgers. "Yeah," he said, slapping the steering wheel, looking along the row of cars beside them, "I'll probably keep this car until next spring, then trade it in on a new one. I'll come out okay that way."

Chris looked around to see if Sally was working. He thought about coming out okay; quitting school, getting a good job, buying a new car. He was not getting paid anything for his work at the station, and he needed money.

Later they cruised up and down 82nd, shouting at girls, laughing. By two, when traffic had thinned, Buzz tried to get things stirred up by betting Murphy that he wouldn't run a red light; Murphy jammed the cigarette to the side of his mouth and took the bet. He slowed down and went through just as the light turned green.

"Sheeut," Buzz said, "that wasn't red."

"Okay, wise guy," Murphy said, and he proceeded to run every red light on 82nd. At each intersection, as they approached the light, Chris felt his stomach tighten, felt the tension grow like a solid element; there was excitement in the danger.

They came through Lents as a false dawn blossomed over the rooftops. Chris, Buzz, and Bill sat on the top of the backseat, high in the sweet morning air, and they were singing like a barbershop trio the single word: *sonsabitch!* They shouted it in chorus, harmonizing, drawing out its syllables. Laughing Chris stood on the backseat as Murphy floorboarded the gas and they sailed through the last intersection without stopping, their song ringing over the empty streets like a joyous challenge: *Sonsabitch!*

The following day, Sunday, the station was closed, Chris slept late, woke slowly, and ate breakfast at noon. He thumbed through old copies of *Hot Rod*, thought about going to Bill's house, thought about going to a movie at the Aero. He made a feeble attempt to clean up his room, picked up a pile of dirty clothes and made his bed, and then went into the garage to look for something to do there. Outside the sky darkened and a heavy rain began to fall; he enjoyed being alone in the garage; sitting on a stack of old tires, hearing the rain on the roof.

His sister spent the afternoon with a girlfriend so there were only three for supper: he and his mother at the table, and his father in the front room. Perhaps it was his sister's absence that accounted for the subdued atmosphere. Chris worked his way through the Sunday paper while he ate, and listened to the programs that came from the floor-model radio beside his father's chair: Fred Allen, The Jack Benny Show, The Whistler. Across from him his mother broke a cracker into her soup, scooped what crumbs fell to the table into her palm and put them into the bowl—nothing wasted that was her motto. Chris suddenly realized she looked older, her face drawn; for almost two months she had been mother, wife, and nurse, and she showed the strain.

The whole house had changed, he thought, going into the front room: it had aged, grown worn, and in spite of the warm weather the room seemed chilly. He saw with new clarity the thread patterns of the rug where the weave showed, the cracked plaster, scuffed furniture. The radio's finger-smoothed knobs and cracked glass dial, the books in the case, the chipped ashtray—familiar things whose shoddiness he had never noticed before.

The chair in which his father sat was growing shapeless. His bathrobe was faded, the ties frayed and knotted; the slippers were cracked at the sides, heels run over, and the material conformed to the lumpy shape of his bone structure. As Chris handed him the main section of the paper he saw that the fine lines around his eyes had deepened and the eyes seemed drawn below the skin; the steely blue pupils were glazed, the whites yellowed. Above Fred Allen's voice and the radio laughter Chris could hear the sound of breathing, like a file pulled against wood. And yet, to his dismay, even now Chris watched his father's fingers nimbly roll a cigarette and light it, saw the flame rise brightly and die in the cloud of smoke. He gave a short cough, picked a fleck of tobacco from his lower lip and drew in more smoke. How innocent that gesture once seemed; he could remember sitting on his father's lap, and laughing with delight as he blew a trail of smoke rings.

"Rub my ankles, willya?"

Chris pretended not to hear; instead he turned to the classifieds and began to study the fine print, as if he intended to buy another car. His father asked again, and when he asked a third time Chris finally looked up, glancing away immediately.

"Naw," he said, "I don't want to." He felt that rubbing his father's ankles was somehow demeaning, perhaps even obscene.

"Oh c'mon, Chris," he said, shifting his body in the chair; he had had so many shots during the past two months that it was terribly painful to remain in the same position for very long. Then, unwillingly, Chris slid across the floor to the hassock which supported his father's feet. The ankles were thick and swollen, the tissue so filled with fluid that the slippers bowed outward; his father kicked off the slippers and Chris began to rub the puffy flesh, hating the fatty tissue which rolled under his skin.

"Ahhh, that's better."

70

Chris sat on the worn rug massaging the ugly flesh; the ankles seemed to belong to someone else, for his father was thin as an axle–and he had the feeling that everything was falling apart.

Later he got in the old Ford and drove alone through his neighborhood; he went down Foster, then drove on side streets, and finally down the roads behind Horace's house which were little better than twin ruts leading nowhere. He drove to a point above Indian Rock and looked out into the darkness. Sunday nights had always depressed him and tonight, as he drove through the rain, things seemed especially gloomy. He saw no one walking, saw few cars; it was as if he had travelled past the edge of an invisible boundary and had set himself adrift in the darkness. That he could see people moving in their houses only made his desperation more acute; they walked through cheerful yellow kitchens with bright curtains, happy and healthy. It seemed to him that their house had been like that only a few months before, and he was amazed how quickly the situation had changed. He drove over the familiar roads feeling terribly depressed and lonely, feeling most of all a self-pity which brought tears to his eyes, not knowing what to do or which way to turn until, as the gas gauge neared empty, he finally turned toward his home.

In the morning he found his life changed, his childish dreams diminished like the stars which faded into the aluminum sky of dawn; this was another level, and someday he would see that life had unfolded like accordian stairs, a series of staggered plateaus that one had to follow upward; there was no going back. He woke to the darkened room, dawn screened beyond the curtains; before he heard his mother's voice he heard the sharp, insistent cry of birds and knew by the clarity of their notes that they flew through the thin air of early morning. His mother called again. Now he was awake, his mind racing past sleep as he slipped into his pants–oh god no, he thought–and in the house the tableau that would forever be burnt into his memory: his mother by the window, silhouetted against the faint light; his sister, awakened by the cries, leaned on a chair, the confusion of the room

71

reflected in her eyes; neither cried nor turned her head from the figure seen through the door's oblique opening.

"He wanted to go to the bathroom," his mother said.

His father was lying on the bedroom floor, face down, one leg bent halfway under as if he were frozen in the position of trying to rise. Chris kneeled beside him, trying to imagine what he could do to reverse this, not allowing himself to think that his father was dead.

"No, listen," he said, and as he rolled his father over a thin rattle came from the throat; the noise repeated itself, and then the room was silent. He laid the limp head back, trying to think what to do: his father had got out of bed headed for the bathroom, and with his wife's help had got this far—that was it. Chris suddenly realized it was all over, and he was amazed later to recall that he had not panicked in the face of this revelation. In fact, he didn't even speak after that short phrase of hope— there was nothing to say. He laid the head back, noticed the short black stubble along his father's chin, the dried spittle in the corner of his mouth like a layer of salt; his eyes were closed but his mouth seemed to be open in the shape of an unsaid word, and the whitish tongue was pushed past teeth. He closed the open pajama fly and left the room, left his father who seemed to be sleeping on the floor. He heard the clicking noise of the telephone as his mother insistently dialed a number.

It was over that fast—a doctor came, the ambulance took away his father's body, and he noticed that the sun was barely over the serrated ridge of pines to the east. Most mornings he would still be asleep at this hour. He asked his mother if she thought he should go to work. She said no.

I'm not crying, he thought. No one is crying.

Later, he was able to know the intensity of the stunned confusion when he would recall absurd things he did or said during those days. At the funeral home he and his sister wandered into an adjoining room, where they saw a luxurious coffin; attracted by its beauty they tiptoed to the plush lining and looked inside, to jump back in horror at the sight of the pale, balding corpse. Or the time when they were driving home from the funeral home and he had remarked that his father had had a good life, that he had not suffered. "I mean," he said, as if he knew anything about life, "he never had his tonsils out or anything like that." An uncle he had seen only once made the supreme gesture and let Chris drive his new car; as they shot down the road the uncle tried to give Chris a pep talk about the meaning of life. The day of the funeral Chris brought in some photos of cars to show to people; was his excitement genuine or feigned? he wondered. After the funeral, when most of the relatives had gone, Chris and another uncle went to a drive-in movie in the old Ford which, at the end of the films, refused to start; they had to wait until the crowd had left, and push it around the empty theater. With an amazement born of the ridiculous or the remarkable that was the tone of the week, a collage of events that seemed marked by extreme clarity but which quickly blurred: later he was to ask whether they had really happened.

For instance, he had the impression that a neighbor had gone with him on the day that his father had died and that they had towed the old Buick home; it had sat in that posh neighborhood for almost three weeks, and no sooner was it home than he and Buzz had taken a sledge hammer to it. The fenders refused to yield to the hammer at first, the thick steel ringing in triumph, but slowly they beat the metal back until it folded against tires and body panels. Were they crazy? he wondered, swinging that ten pound hammer with all his strength, as if working off anger and sorrow.

After everyone was gone, he remembered, the three who were now the family joined to make a final gesture: they flew a kite. This playfulness was somewhat out of character for the mother, yet it must have been her idea. Certainly neither Chris nor his sister cared about kites; but then where had it come from? The fragile blue and yellow simplicity of paper and balsa, lettered with store advertising, was already assembled by someone, and they carried it to the vacant lot across the street. The mother knew nothing of the mechanics of flight, yet she took the first run; she held the string and her feet and skirt

73

stammered as she galloped across the field to the far edge and back to where Chris and his sister waited, the kite cartwheeling like an enraged beast. Then Chris took a turn, although he felt gawky and odd running across the high grass; the kite teased with a slight ascent before it dropped into the skirt of grass.

The tail was too short; no stability. There was no breeze. Or, most likely, the spirit of kiting was absent.

The sister was too young, her legs too short, so all three grabbed handholds and ran furiously, the child and the kite being dragged along. The kite lifted to telephone wire height and they moved back slowly; they watched the hovering blue and yellow diamond, as delicate as a moth, and they turned to one another to share this success.

While Chris felt a cold satisfaction at this accomplishment he was startled when the mother began to laugh wildly; his sister giggled, then also laughed until she had to hold her side with one hand.

Then the breeze lessened and the kite shot down at an abrupt plane, the product of a medieval catapult. They were at the field's edge and in mild panic each moved in a separate direction, each trying to jerk the string and break the kite's descent; then, confused, they moved together again, to mill in a lumbering circle dance. The shadow of the kite darkened them as it passed like a premonition; they were a crowd of arms and legs at all angles as the loops of string fell, and they were hopelessly bound together by the snarl of cord as the kite smashed with puny finality at their feet.

That was in some ways only a prelude to the summer: he burned off the rest of the Ford's clutch lining and when that car refused to move he abandoned it. He took the battery and license plates and put them on a 1938 Olds tudor which he got from the field behind the station; that lasted less than a week, when its primitive Hydra-Matic went out. A Studebaker Commander coupe blew an engine the second day; a 1938 Ford threw a rod through the side of the block; a Chevrolet coupe scattered its transmission along Foster when, in sadness and anger, he tried to speed shift to second. He drove with increasing frenzy, wasting cars one after the other, until it was difficult for him to drive down a road without seeing a car that he had left behind. It surprised him that he had no regrets.

He thought that he had learned something about the impermanence of metal and flesh, but he hadn't—not until years later could he even begin to know what his father knew as he fell through that fragile membrane. What the death meant to Chris was the absence of his father; the empty chair at the table, the missing voice when he wanted someone to talk with, the problem of what to do with the father's razor, underwear, neckties. He missed the man's presence. He would recall their stops at the ice cream store: in a hovering image he would come out with cones and see his father through the car window, his face dark against the glass like a cameo, and he would suddenly be saddened to think that the ice cream cone had become his father's single pleasure. Remembering specific moments, he would regret not having put an arm around his father, not having told him that he loved him: that was the material of dreams, where he would meet his father in stores, on the street, at the homes of friends, and they would talk about all the things that they had never had a chance to discuss.

Not until years later could he begin to understand what his father must have felt; betrayed by his body, pounding heart, softening muscles. What had it cost him to ask others to do his work? "Doc said I wasn't supposed to lift anything heavy," he had said, and "I keep having to pee," he had said—these weren't complaints, they were cries of explanation, an appeal that others understand what he could not understand. The bitter moment when he stood beside the old Ford saying "I can't, I can't push it;" how could Chris hope to know the panic his father knew when he found his body disobeying, when he suddenly found he was too weak to do the work he had done all his life—and it was terrifying because this weakness was translated into failure. "If you don't work," he had always said, "you don't eat."

75

Those lessons came later; if he learned anything from the death at the time it was to recognize his own mortality. It terrified him to realize that his father was only slightly more than twice Chris' age when he died, and he tried to project a span of years equal to the number he had lived; he felt that he had hardly begun to live and as he listened to his heart beating against ribs, he thought that a lifetime was awfully brief.

About the Author

Albert Drake was born in Portland, Oregon when it was less populous and life had the quality of Norman Rockwell paintings. He was educated in public schools and followed his father's footsteps, working for years in service stations, garages and automotive warehouses. He eventually attended Portland State College, and got his degrees at the University of Oregon. He twice won the Ernest Haycox Prize for fiction. For nearly 30 years he labored in the groves of academe, where he was cited for his outstanding teaching and rose to the rank of Full Professor. He was the first academic to teach a class in science fiction as literature, and for several years he was Director of the Clarion Science Fiction Workshop. He has received numerous academic and creative grants, including two major grants from the National Endowment for the Arts. His fiction, poetry and prose have been widely published in literary quarterlies and popular magazines, including *Redbook*, *Epoch*, *North American Review* and *The Best American Short Stories*. He is currently Professor Emeritus of English.

Books by Albert Drake

Poetry
Michigan Signatures (Ed) (1969)
Riding Bike (1973)
Cheap Thrills (1975)
Rustfire (1975)
Returning to Oregon (1975)
Garage (1981)
Homesick (1988)

Fiction
The Postcard Mysteries (1975)
Tillamook Burn (1977)
In the Time of Surveys (1978)
I Remember the Day James Dean Died (1983)

Novels
One Summer (1979)
Beyond the Pavement (1981)

Non-Fiction
Street Was Fun in '51 (1982)
The Big "Little GTO" Book (1982)
A 1950's Rod & Custom Builder's Wishbook (1985)
Herding Goats (1989)
Hot Rodder!: From Lakes to Street (1993)
Flat Out (1994)
Fifties Flashback (1998)
Portland Pictorial: The 1950s (2006)
Northwest Oldtimers (2007)
Age of Hot Rods (2008)
Jacket & Plaque (2008)
Christmas at Ed's Richfield (2009)
Overtures to Motion (2011)

www.flatoutpress.com